The Rare Book Press

Presents …

The Fabled Journal

of

Beauty

By Boyd Brent

Author contact: boyd.brent1@gmail.com

D1367320

Journal entry no. 1

I'm *actually* doing this. Keeping a journal. Something that's strictly forbidden in the land of fairytales. I don't suppose the idea of doing so was even supposed to occur to me. But I heard through the grapevine that Snow White's been keeping one. Apparently, not only has it allowed her to tell the truth about her life but also to resolve her many issues. It's common knowledge throughout the land that Snow has struggled to get to grips with her fairest of them all status. But that knowledge was *never* supposed to reach the real world in The Lost Diary of Snow White. Far be it from me to trump a fellow fairytale character, but if Snow imagines she has a lot to live up to being known as the fairest in the land, then she should consider what it's like being called Beauty. I think you'll agree that no matter how firmly a mother believes her baby to be the most beautiful ever born, she would never dream of naming her Beauty. All mothers assume, quite rightly, that such a name would be a lot to live up to. Imagine if your parents had called you Beauty, and you had no surname to dilute it? How awkward might you feel being introduced to strangers? I'm actually grateful that I don't have a surname, as it would undoubtedly have been Personified or Incarnate. I suppose it is easier to deal with a name like Beauty in the land of fairytales, where names that double as sweeping statements are commonplace. My hands are trembling at the thought of being caught making my first entry. I will find a hiding place for it, but I am resolved to return to it tomorrow. It's so liberating!

Journal entry no. 2

It is the eve of the following day, and I have felt anxious about my first journal entry and yet excited at the prospect of my second in equal measure. Okay, deep breath; in for a penny, in for a pound. What I am about to commit to paper is forbidden to even *think* about, let alone write down. But here goes … with a name like Beauty, I have often wondered what the title of my story might be. If you're in possession of my completed journal, then you'll be reading these words in the future when its name is commonplace. You'll, therefore, be aware if the following ideas on the subject are correct. Earlier today, while out walking in the woods with my best friend Betty, she whispered the following suggestions: "What about, 'Beauty & The *Most* Charming Prince?' Or 'Beauty and the Most *Gallant* Charming?' Oh, I know! What about 'Beauty and the Frog Who Is Transformed into the Most Splendid of Princes?'" she pondered.

"I suppose they're all possibilities," I replied, "although that last one sounds a little long-winded." Betty has always been so positive and upbeat about things. She's a scullery maid in my father's household, and we grew up together. I have heard through the grapevine how the truth about our fairytale lives gets blurred by endless re-telling. I therefore have *no* idea if she'll be mentioned in my story when it reaches the real world. So, and from the horse's mouth, Betty is not only my best friend but a genuine beauty where it counts: on the inside. As we made our way back from the woods this afternoon, she placed her hands on her ample hips, scratched at the mole on her nose and said, "Perhaps your story will simply be called 'Beauty?'"

As kindly as it was meant, I shuddered at her suggestion. "Your guess is as good as mine, Betty. Indeed, I hope your guess is a good deal better."

"Why do you say so?"

"Just a feeling I have. A sort of dark foreboding."

"You never know," smiled Betty with a chuckle, "maybe your story will be called 'Beauty and Betty?'"

"Now that's a lovely idea!" I said, placing an arm around her shoulder.

When we arrived home, I was informed by the footman that a family meeting was underway and that I should make my presence known in the parlour without delay.

When I entered the parlour, the expressions that greeted me were so grim that I imagined my journal had been discovered. Father was sat at the head of the table, while my three brothers and two sisters were seated on either side of him. I headed for my seat beside my sisters, chin held high and determined to put my case for keeping a journal. I should explain that while my brothers are perfectly lovely, my sisters, as I believe is quite common in fairytales, can be somewhat jealous at times. Hardly surprising when you consider how they must endure having a sister called Beauty. And, unlike Snow White, I can see how my reflection fits a certain ideal of what is considered beautiful. Although, where this 'ideal' springs from, goodness only knows. But I digress; so, back to the topic of my sisters ...

The reason for the above dots is this: I had intended to write their names but drew a blank. It seems that not only must they suffer my being called *Beauty*, but that the original Author has declined to give them names of their own. Ditto my brothers. Only now does it make perfect sense why I have always referred to them all as 'Darling sister' or 'Brother of mine.' Cripes. It's little wonder keeping a diary is forbidden if such things can come to light so easily.

"Glad you could join us," huffed one of my sisters as I sat beside her.

"It's about time. Where on earth have you been? Father has something important he wants to tell us," said the other.

"I was out walking with Betty."

"*Again*?" tutted a sister. "That girl is as low born as she is simple."

"Indeed, our sister's time would be better spent conversing with a cabbage."

"Come now, Darling Sisters, there's no need to be unpleasant," I said.

Father smiled at me. "Dear Beauty, you have always had a place in your heart for waifs and strays."

"Betty's hardly a waif *or* a stray, Father."

"No. Indeed, she's a fine and upstanding member our household," said one of my brothers, to which the other two concurred with a well-intentioned "Here, here!"

One of my sisters folded her arms. "I presume you haven't called this family meeting to discuss *Betty*, Father?"

"No. Indeed, I have not. But wish I had, for the news is not good," he said miserably.

"*Please* tell us you're not going to restrict our allowance again this month?" pleaded a sister.

"He simply *can't*," said the other, "it's going to be a struggle buying new gowns for the coming season as it is."

Father took off his glasses, placed them on the table and wiped a tear from his eye.

"Whatever is the matter? I asked, reaching across the table and squeezing his hand.

"There is no easy way to soften the blow, so I will just come out and say it … there has been an accident at sea, a *terrible* loss of life."

"Anyone we know?" said one of my sisters as though she couldn't understand what all the fuss was about.

"No, no one we know, but that's hardly a comfort," said Father, taking a hanky from his pocket and blowing his nose.

One of my sisters stood abruptly. "Well, if that's all, Papa, I have an appointment with my manicurist."

"No. That is not all," sighed Father.

My sister lowered herself back onto her chair.

"My fortune …" he began.

"What of it?" asked one of my sisters impatiently.

"It has sunk to the bottom of the sea with those poor sailors. Our wealth is gone. We are poor."

"*Poor*? Then what's to become of us?" asked an ashen faced sister.

"Take heart, my children. It's not all bad news," said Father, putting a brave face on things, "for once we've sold everything we own, and I have paid off my debtors, we will have enough to buy a small cottage in the country. Once there, we can live happy yet frugal lives."

"Frugal!" exclaimed one of my sisters as though it were a terminal disease.

Father brushed some lint from the table and nodded.

As my sisters wept into their hands, I stood up and placed my arms around his shoulders. "It will be all right," I said, "after all, we still have each other, and the fresh air will do us good."

One of my sisters looked up from her tear-sodden palms. "Do us GOOD!" she bellowed. "What good can possibly come from living like peasants!"

"It will doubtless be difficult at first," said Father, "but in time, I'm sure we'll all grow accustomed to it."

It was at this point that my sisters said some words that have no place in this journal. So, I have found no place for them.

Journal entry no. 3

A horse and cart arrived today to convey my sisters'
belongings to auction. They are to be sold off, as is all the
furniture in this grand house. Father will use the proceeds to
buy our cottage. I sat at my bedroom window, chin on palm,
and watched three men take over an hour to convey my
sisters' dresses from the house to their cart. As for myself, I
have never been one to covert possessions and own very
little. So, it's probably a good thing that I am rumoured to be
a main character and have what is best described as my main
character's outfit—a lovely blue and white dress that's as
figure hugging as it is self-cleaning. As for accessories, I
have a simple silver bracelet with matching necklace. Even
so, not wishing to be singled out for any favouritism, and
eager to do my bit to help Father, I went into town today
with the intention of selling them both. Our town is typical of
those found in fairytales: Tudor style shops and houses with
thick wooden beams, thatched roofs, and window boxes
where flowers are always in bloom. There are fountains,
maypoles, and townsfolk always amiable going about their
business. I made my way down the main thoroughfare, and it
wasn't long before Philip made himself known. The poor boy
has had a crush on me for as long as I can remember. He's a
nice young man, tall, dark and loyal, who could have his pick
of girls. But I've never had any romantic feelings for him.
Betty once suggested that I kiss him. "You never know, he

might transform into someone who makes me go weak at the knees," she said. Unfortunately, when I planted an unexpected kiss on his cheek, it was Philip who grew weak and staggered sideways. But back to today …

"Beauty!" said Philip, whipping out a bunch of flowers. "These are for you."

"Thank you, Philip. They're beautiful," I replied, taking and sniffing them.

"A mere trifle. Indeed, their beauty pales in comparison with your own."

"It's kind of you to say so. Although they are more fragrant."

"You jest," said Philip, twirling the ends of his moustache.

I shook my head. "They're *roses, Philip.*"

"I know. The lady in the shop was at great pains to point that out. So," he went on, inhaling heartily and offering me his arm, "where are you off to on this fine morning?"

"To the pawn shop to sell my necklace," I said, feeling for its familiar presence with the tips of my fingers.

"But why?" he asked as we began walking.

"The news is not good; poor Father's fortunes have taken a turn for the worse. I am intent on doing my bit to help him."

Philip's broadening smile seemed at odds with my news. I was about to inquire what had amused him so when he said, "You need only agree to marry me, and you can keep your necklace."

His proposal caught me unawares, and I began to cough. "It's … it's kind of you to offer, Philip, but … I really don't think that's how my story is supposed to end."

"End?" he said, throwing his arms wide. "It would be just the beginning!"

"Yes, of the end …" I murmured under my breath.

"What?"

"Nothing."

Philip raised his chin. "Whatever the pawn merchant offers you, I'll double it."

"You like my necklace and bracelet *that* much?"

"I do."

"But they would neither fit *nor* suit you, Philip," I pointed out.

"No, I …"

"I'm joking."

"I knew that. They'll make fine additions to my collection of Beauty things."

Okay. Not at all creepy. "What Beauty things?" I asked and regretted doing so instantly.

"Well, there's the hair that I removed from your sleeve when …"

"Really? You kept that?"

"Of course, I kept it," he said, inflating his chest. "Then there's the tissue you discarded when you had that dreadful cold …"

"You went *back* for it?"

Philip nodded. "Does this dedication not prove the length and breadth of my love?"

"It proves something, Philip. Look," I told him for the umpteenth time, "you really *must* seek a wife elsewhere. And not waste a moment more on me."

"I know you don't mean that," he said with the usual dulled twinkle in his eye. It's not Philip's fault he can't see sense when it comes to me. It's just the way he was written. "I can assure that I do mean it. And here is the pawn shop."

"My offer still stands. I will *double* whatever he offers you."

"Save your money for things you *need*, Philip. Things of use," I said, disappearing through the door into the shop.

When I returned home and gave Father the money from the sale, he wept miserably. "I cannot accept this! You must return to the shop this instant and buy them back."

"Don't be silly, Father. At a time like this, your need is greater than mine."

"But they were your only things of worth."

"Nonsense. I have the love of a kindly father, which is priceless."

"As ever, you make me so proud, and I promise to make it up to you," he sighed.

"Make it up to *her*?" came the disgruntled voice of one of my sisters as they entered the room.

"You would lament Beauty's *pitiful* sacrifice? When your other daughters have been forced to give up so much," said the other.

"It is because Beauty had so little that her sacrifice is so great," Father pointed out.

"Oh, that's right; take her side. You always do." An awkward silence followed, broken by a servant who entered the room and presented Father with a letter upon a silver tray. Doubtless expecting more bad news, Father observed the letter under his nose as though it smelled rotten. He shrugged, picked it up and ripped it open.

"What is it now?" said one of my sisters, rolling her eyes. "Are we to give up the very clothes on our backs?"

Father smiled. "No. It's nothing of the sort … in fact, it's good news!"

"Good news? Really? Has a rich relative died and left us a fortune?" asked one of my sisters, crossing her fingers.

"No, they have not," replied Father testily over the top of the letter.

"Then what is it?" I asked.

"Apparently, not all of my ships were lost in that storm after all. Indeed, one has made it back to port laden with riches!"

Father jumped to his feet. "It seems I must leave immediately to claim its cargo."

"God's speed, Father!" said one of my sisters, opening the door for him.

"Allow me to fetch your coat," said the other, darting into the hall.

Father and I followed my sisters into the hallway.

"I shall be gone for several days," said Father, pulling on his coat, "what gifts would you like me to bring you back?"

Having glanced at one another, my sisters plunged their hands into their pockets. "It just so happens that we have already made lists."

"*Already?*" said Father, raising an eyebrow.

"Yes. They're intended for our future suitors. Why wait to make them?"

"Why indeed," sighed Father, taking the lists. He placed his hat on his head and looked at me. "What would you like your papa to bring back for you, Beauty?"

"Oh, you know me, Father. What do I always ask you for whenever you go away?"

"A single rose?"

I nodded. "A single rose."

Journal entry no. 4

Father has been away for three days and nights now. Not a great deal has happened since he left. The house has been so quiet. My sisters have spent their days in town, spreading the news of our good fortune. As for my brothers, shortly after packing their own frugal possessions onto a cart for sale, they went off to find work in the country. We have sent word of our change in fortune but don't yet know if they have received it. As for me, my days have passed in contemplation about what the future might hold and engaging in my favourite pastime of reading. I have only left the house to borrow and return books to the library. I adore books and can't imagine a better way to pass the time than by travelling to far-flung places and losing myself in the trials and tribulations of others. Today, after visiting the library, I met Betty for a beverage in the Ye Old Storyteller's Tea Shop. As soon as she saw me stumble through the door of that establishment laden with several thick volumes, she rushed over and unburdened me of a good many. "Oh, thank you, Betty!"

"I have no idea how you get through so many books …" said Betty, hugging the tonnes to her ample bosom. She hurried back to our table and plonked them down.

"I suppose that having no gainful employment of my own has allowed my love for reading to flourish," I replied, following her.

"Some might say to get out of control," said Betty.

"Yes, I suppose they might, but reading is good for the soul. I wish you'd meet me *at* the library for once. Truly, it is a wonderful place," I said, taking my seat beside her.

Betty shook her head adamantly. "The library's too grand for the likes of me."

"I can assure you that it isn't. Books are for *everyone*."

"Yes. Well, that sounds all well and good, but what use have I for books when I can't read?"

"But I've been teaching you."

"And very grateful I am, too, but I don't think I was written that way. As a reader, I mean. I keep forgetting everything you teach me."

I squeezed Betty's hand. "The land of fairytales can be a cruel place."

"No need to remind me of that," said Betty, picking at the scabs on her calloused hands. "When the messenger brought word that your papa had lost his fortune, I wondered what was to become of me."

I smiled. "Take heart, for he will return soon, having salvaged a goodly part of it."

Betty placed her elbows on the table and rested her chin in her hands. "Your sisters must have been *thrilled* by the news."

I nodded wholeheartedly. "You're not wrong. They have given Father a list of presents to bring them back."

"I just bet they have."

"Don't be unkind," I said, lowering my voice, "my sisters were just written that way."

"Speaking of which," said Betty, rolling her eyes, "I don't suppose I need ask what you asked your papa for?"

"You need not. Obviously, a rose. I just couldn't help myself. To be honest, I would have preferred some books."

"Then why didn't you ask for books?"

"I had every intention of doing so, but when I opened my mouth, I heard myself confirm that I wanted a rose."

"Written that way?" sighed Betty.

"Apparently so." I glanced about to see if anyone might be listening to our conversation. The coffee shop was frequented by the usual patrons: animated ladies gossiping, men reading the Daily Tale newspaper, and the old Mr Whiskers asleep before the fire. I leaned in close and whispered in Betty's ear, "I have the strangest feeling that a rose is central to my story."

"Beauty and The Rose?" mused Betty.

I grabbed her arm. "We should not talk of such things here."

"Right, you are," she replied, glancing left and right.

On our way home, we were ambushed by Philip who insisted on taking the books I was carrying. "... Well, if you must," I said.

"I absolutely must," he replied, wrestling them from my grasp.

"And what about Betty's?"

"Don't mind me, I'll be fine ..." said Betty, stumbling a little.

"You heard her. She's built like an ox. What do you intend to do with all these doorstoppers anyhow?"

"Charming. And they're not doorstoppers; they're *books*, and I intend to read them."

"*All* of them?"

"Yes, Phillip. Stories engage my imagination and transport me to places I would otherwise never go. There is nothing quite like seeing the world, often other worlds, through the eyes of others."

"And the point of this out-of-body gazing would be?"

"So that I might share in adventures and learn from them."

"You could learn all you need to know from me," said Phillip.

"It's very kind of you to offer but ..."

"But Beauty already knows everything you do and a good deal more besides," chuckled Betty.

"I suggest you hold your tongue, scullery maid, or …"

Betty somehow managed to balance her books in one hand and hold her tongue with her other. "'ike is you mean."

Philip stopped walking, and his cheeks glowed with rage.

"I'll take these, that's if you don't mind," I said, wrestling the books away from him.

"Very well, but I suggest you have a word with your servant," he said, brushing down the lapels of his frockcoat with the back of his hands.

"I'll do no such thing. Betty's my friend. And I encourage my friends to speak their minds. And now we will bid you a good day." We walked away, leaving Philip open-mouthed on a street corner.

Journal entry no. 5

Earlier today, when Father returned from his quest to claim his ship's cargo, his mood was difficult to read. To the delight of my sisters, he arrived home in a golden carriage laden with luxuries that made them swoon. At first, I imagined his trip must have been a great success. But as I observed him, his expression gave me cause for concern: one moment he was smiling at the reaction of two of his children to his rediscovered wealth, and the next, well, if I'm perfectly honest, he looked rather guilty. If I didn't know Father better, I might have suspected him of skulduggery, of stealing the carriage from a rich merchant. And when he approached me with a red rose, quite unable to make eye contact, my suspicions grew. "Thank you … it's beautiful, Father," I said, taking the rose. "You've obviously been successful in your quest," I continued, glancing towards the open top carriage where my sisters swarmed like bees on a honeycomb.

Father nodded and wiped the sweat from his brow.

"What is it? What's wrong?" I asked him.

"Oh, dear Beauty!" he exclaimed with heartfelt passion. "Ever since you were little, it has felt as though you could see into my very soul!" My sisters froze and looked over at us. "Papa? Is something the matter?"

"Yes, Papa. These treasures *do* belong to us, don't they?" asked the other, admiring the jewel-encrusted ring she'd just slipped on her finger.

"Yes, they belong to us *but* …" Father shuddered so violently that I took him by the arm and led him towards the house. In the entrance hall, the servants had arranged themselves in a line to welcome him home. One took his hat; another his coat; and a third, his cane. "Now come into the parlour and explain why you have such a ghostly pallor," I said, leading him in that direction.

In the parlour, Father slumped into his favourite armchair and, having placed his head against its rest, gazed wide-eyed at the ceiling. "Where to begin …" he murmured.

I pulled up a chair and sat beside him. "Like the best stories, at the *beginning*. You went to the docks and found your ship?"

Father closed his eyes and nodded.

"And it was laden with all the treasures you have returned with?"

Father opened his eyes and, meeting my gaze for the first time, shook his head. "The ship's hold did contain a great many luxuries but …"

"But what?"

"It also contained my debtors who were taking stock of the ship's inventory. Once they had removed what I owed them, I was left with *nothing*."

"Nothing? Then how have you returned in a golden carriage laden with so much treasure?"

"Where to begin," he said, miserably.

"At the *beginning*," I repeated.

Father sighed. "I was on my way home with the sad news that I knew would disappoint my family …"

"You're such a caring person; it's little wonder the thought of returning home with such news made you miserable."

"Caring, you say? Caring she calls me!"

"But you have *always* been so …" I said, taking his shaky hands in my own.

"Oh, dear Beauty. I fear that if what I encountered on my way home was a test of that caring, then I have failed it."

"What makes you say such things?"

Father got a faraway look in his eyes. "I … I got lost ..."

"*Lost*? But the route must be so familiar to you."

"It is. But on this occasion, I came across an unexpected fork in the road, and a choice had to be made."

"And where did your choice lead you?"

"To a palace."

"*Palace*? To my knowledge, there are no palaces between here and the docks."

"That's what I would have said before I came upon it."

"Are you certain it was a palace? Maybe it was a very grand villa."

Father shook his head. "It was the biggest, grandest palace you can imagine, Beauty, and …"

"And?"

"And I was cold and hungry, and its front doors were open wide as though in welcome."

"You went inside?"

Father nodded. "At first, I stood just inside the door and called out, 'Hello? Is anyone home?' There was no reply. I could see a lit fireplace in a room just across the main hall. My hands felt as though they were frozen and so I … I made my way through the hall into the room and warmed them before the fire."

"And still you saw no one?"

"Not a soul. Even though the palace was spotless and clearly somebody's home. The room I'd entered was a dining room and, while its table was long enough to seat a hundred guests, it was laid for just one."

"How curious," I said, taping my lower lip.

"That's what I thought. And what's more, the place setting was surrounded by dishes filled with delicious food."

"I see," I said, sitting back in my seat.

"As I said, the palace was deserted, and it seemed a shame to let all that food go to waste …"

"Well," I said optimistically, "I'm sure the owner of such a grand palace would not begrudge a weary traveller something to eat. Is that why you look so guilty?"

"If only it were!" he replied, gripping the arms of his chair.

I cleared my throat nervously. "So … tell me; what happened next?"

"After my meal, I felt tired and lay down on a sofa. I fell asleep and awoke the next morning feeling refreshed and determined to complete my journey home."

"But that doesn't explain the riches you've returned with," I said, motioning to the window.

Father placed his hands over his eyes and muttered miserably to himself.

"Father? You're making me nervous."

He lowered his hand and gazed at the rose in my hand. "As I was leaving," he began, "I noticed a magnificent rose garden, and remembering the promise I had made you, I reasoned, *What harm could it do to pick one for my daughter?*"

"And was this the rose?" I said, breathing in its delightful scent.

Father swallowed. "Indeed, it was."

"Such a lovely gesture," I smiled.

"I somehow doubt you'll think so when I tell you what happened next …"

I straightened my back and braced myself for whatever had caused Father to turn so pale.

"*That's* when it happened!" he blurted as though in a spasm.

"That's when *what* happened?"

"The Beast appeared! As if from nowhere!"

"*Beast*?"

"Yes! A monstrous creature as ugly as you are beautiful! It stood nine feet tall, and although it was dressed in a fine suit of clothes, its face and claws were those of a savage fiend! The thing was enraged, and I feared it would tear me limb from limb!"

"Father! What had vexed the creature so?"

Father closed his eyes, calmed his breathing and said, "It *told* me what had vexed it …"

"It could speak?"

"Speak? Not what I'd call it. Certainly, it could bellow or, should I say, ROAR. "'How dare you repay my generosity this way!' it roared with a ferocity that made me cower before it like a naughty child. 'I have provided you with a fire upon which to warm yourself, a feast to quell your hunger, and a couch upon which to sleep.'

'And I am eternally grateful!' I replied as I shrunk backwards in fear for my life.

'Then why have you repaid my generosity by stealing a rose from my garden?' it bellowed, swiping at the air with one of its great paws.

I leant forwards and took hold of Father's Forearm. "Surely, a creature that lives in such a palace would not begrudge you a single rose. Particularly given its earlier generosity."

"You would think so but … but the punishment it was resolved to inflict for my 'crime' …" Father fell silent.

"What punishment?"

"Death!"

I shuddered so hard that the rose fell from my hand upon the carpet. "For picking a rose?"

Father closed his eyes and nodded. "It told me that my only hope was to plead my case. To explain my actions."

"And what was your defence? It must have been convincing, for you have returned to us safe and sound."

Father opened his eyes, scratched at his chin and said, "I told the Beast that the rose was intended to be a gift for one of my three daughters—the most beautiful young woman you can imagine, not only in her appearance but also in nature."

I felt myself blushing.

"And while," continued Father, "my other two daughters had requested that I bring them back fine clothes and jewellery, the daughter in question asked only that I return with a single rose. I told the Beast that I did not see the harm in taking one, not when it had so many. And you can imagine my relief when my words appeared to calm the creature. Indeed, it listened most attentively to my explanation."

"And took pity on you?"

"What makes you say so?"

"You are home, Father."

"Yes, but not before I had promised it what it asked for in return for my freedom."

My curiosity was joined by a dark foreboding which must have been conveyed by my expression, for Father answered it: "To escape with my life, I had no option but to promise the Beast that what it asked for in return …"

"Which was?"

"*You*," shuddered Father.

"Me? But I don't understand."

"The Beast said it would let me go, spare my life if the daughter for whom the rose was intended took my place."

I sprang to my feet, the room spinning around me.

"*No!*" said Father, reaching out and taking my hands in his own. "You don't have to go. It doesn't know where we live. And what's more, such a hideous creature must stay hidden for fear of being hunted and killed. Why else has no one ever seen it?"

I reached down and placed a comforting hand upon Father's head. "The Beast would have killed you had you not agreed to its terms. I cannot think of anything that would have pained me more than losing you in such a way. Don't you see? You had no *choice*. Just as I have none now."

Father gazed up at me with tears in his eyes. "Your desire to *always* do the right thing by others be blasted to smithereens," he said, holding my hand to his tear sodden cheek.

"Take heart, Father, for I have done nothing to this creature. Committed no crime in its eyes. It is, therefore, unlikely it wants to hurt me. I will go and talk to it. Reason with it." It was then that the door to the parlour fell open, and my sisters spilt into the room. They stood before us, and having mustered as much dignity as a pair of earwiggers might, one said, "I agree with Beauty."

"We both do," said the other, "this Beast can hold no grudge against her. Maybe it is simply desirous of a conversation."

Father shook his head. "The agreement was that Beauty would remain with it as its captive."

Despite their best efforts, my sisters could not help smiling.

I dragged my gaze from them. "His captive?" I murmured.

One of my sisters stepped closer. "But the creature is yet to meet you. And will doubtless tire of you sooner rather than later. And what's more, if Beauty does *not* go to it, it might seek the return of its treasure."

"It's true," said Father regretfully, "the Beast did provide the wagon filled with riches. It told me it would be unfair to return with a rose for Beauty and yet deprive my other daughters the things they had asked for."

"How generous this Beast is!" said one of my sisters.

"Yes, very generous," I said, "and now, if you'll excuse me, I feel suddenly tired." I turned and walked unsteadily to the door.

"Beauty," said Father from behind me, "you do not have to go. It's not as though the Beast's request is in any way just."

My sisters drew breath audibly to disagree.

"Then, why do I feel that I *must*?" I replied over my shoulder.

I returned to my room, placed my back against the wall and slid to the ground as my legs gave way beneath me. I suppose I must have fainted, for some time later, I felt a hand upon my shoulder and heard Betty's reassuring voice. "Beauty? Beauty? Why are you sleeping on the floor?"

I opened my eyes and, seeing my dear friend, threw my arms around her shoulders and whispered, "I know the name of my story!"

"Why do you tremble so?"

"Because I fear that its name is *Beauty and the Beast*!"

"Why would you say such a thing!?"

"Father has just returned from the Beast's palace, and his liberty, his *life* was only spared because he promised that I would take his place."

Betty shook her head. "I don't believe it. Your father is a good man. A *kind* man. He loves you dearly and would never promise such a thing."

"Maybe. Under normal circumstances. But these circumstances were far from normal. The Beast … it terrified him so much that he would have promised it *anything* if it spared his life. And in his fearful state, he convinced himself that whatever he did promise would *not* have to fulfilled."

"Well then, maybe your papa has a point."

I shook my head. "A promise is a promise, particularly when it's made in a land such as this."

"You're *going,* then? To the Beast's home?"

I clambered to my feet. "Yes."

"Then I will go with you!"

I placed a hand upon her shoulder. "Thank you for offering, but I would not place you in danger so needlessly for anything in this world."

Journal entry no 6.

During the hours that followed, my mind conjured such an array of hideous fates at the Beast's hands I decided that for the sake of my sanity, I must leave without delay to discover the truth. Having made up my mind, and being filled with wretched anticipation, I threw some necessities into a bag. Then, readying myself for the happy go lucky performance of my life, I presented myself in the parlour as a traveller off on nothing more than an adventure to the countryside. The open-mouthed expressions that greeted me suggested that my family believed I had lost my marbles. In truth, it felt as though if I did not confront and plead with this *creature* sooner rather than later, I would lose them.

"How ... commendable," smiled one of my sisters.

Father stood up and approached me. "What's this? You mean to go *now*?"

"Yes, Father. To be honest, since I heard I would be going on this, this *adventure*, I've been chomping at the bit to set off …"

"Brave as well as beautiful," replied Father, welling up.

I straightened my back. "Please tell my brothers that I said goodbye and that I love them dearly. And that they must not do anything rash …"

"Yes, of course. They can be hot-headed; I will impress upon them the futility of challenging such a creature."

I nodded. "Thank you. I mean to leave *now*."

"Yes, yes, of course. I know with all my heart that you will charm the Beast," said Father, hugging me close.

"I mean to do my best. Now tell me, how am I to reach my destination?"

"I am reliably informed that the horse that conveyed me home knows the way back …"

"Excellent!" said one of my sisters. "And now we've emptied the carriage of all our presents, there'll be plenty of room for you."

"That was my thinking …" I reached down to pick up my little bag, but Father got there first and then offered me his arm. I clung to it as we made our way outside to Beast's carriage.

Father stood tearful yet stoic as I made myself comfortable inside. Meanwhile, my sisters, huddled together by the front door, struggled to conceal their delight.

"Fear not, Father, for you have raised a strong and independent daughter … one quite up to the task of dealing with whatever this land might throw at her."

Father nodded and smiled as best he could. "You *will* come back to us, Beauty. I know you will."

I glanced at the only home I had ever known, the place I had always felt secure and happy and, seeing Betty's hand pressed to an upstairs window, felt my resolve begin to crumble. "… And now I must be going." As though it heard me, the horse set off for its home, and as much as I would have liked to look back, I dared not.

The carriage wended its way down narrow country lanes where fields of emerald green rolled far into the distance, and lambs grazed without a care. "What could there possibly be to fear on such a lovely day?" I told myself.

I should know by now not to ask such questions, as before very long, the bright cheeriness of the day had been crowded out by darkening skies. What is more, a forest sprung up from *nowhere* and encroached upon the carriage like an inquisitive creature. I gazed into the forest's canopy where it looked as though the uppermost branches of the trees were coming together to shut out the light. "It's grown so cold," I shuddered, condensation leaving my lips. I hugged myself for warmth and, at the sound of howling wolves, huddled as far back in my seat as I could. The fear of a ravenous wolf leaping over the side of the carriage and devouring me goes some way to explaining why my first glimpse of the palace was not entirely unwelcome. In its eagerness to get home, the horse quickened its pace, and before long, the palace was revealed to me in all its eerie beauty. Let's be honest, eeriness and beauty are not natural bedfellows, but this vision of a dark fairytale palace was exactly that: its turrets, once pastel coloured and resplendent, had faded to grey and now wilted as though from sorrow. Its windows, too numerous to count and that once upon a time must have reflected the sun for miles around, were shuttered and filthy with grime. Indeed, the palace had a look of such bewildering sadness about it that it brought a lump to my throat.

As we drew near, the palace's gates opened as though having sensed our approach. And once we had passed through them, their creaking as they closed gave me goosebumps. The carriage came to a halt on the palace's forecourt, and as I looked nervously in the direction of its imposing front door, it, too, began to open. I braced myself for the outline of a person, no, a *Beast* to appear in the illuminated rectangle. No one appeared, and my attention was taken by the sound of the horse's bridal being unbuckled. I rose in my seat for a look at the person doing this and, seeing no one, sat back down and swallowed hard as the horse was led away from the carriage by an invisible *something*. A chill wind picked up and seemed to nudge me in the direction of that rectangle of light. I stood, picked up my little bag and climbed down upon the pebbled forecourt. With my hair blowing in my face like tic-a-tape, I made my way up the steps and, following a brief hesitation, stepped through the front door.

I found myself in a palatial entrance hall where a staircase swept away in two directions to the floor above. A sparkling chandelier, easily the size of the carriage I had just alighted, hung down from the ceiling. Unlike the exterior, the interior of the palace was clearly tended by a great many servants. This realisation that I was not alone with the Beast was a comfort of sorts.

The walls were hung with a great many portraits, but my gaze was drawn by one in particular. It hung above a fireplace on the far-right where the light from candles in sconces on either side cast a luminous glow upon its sitter—a beautiful young man with dark wavy hair. His comeliness, coupled with his look of profound melancholy, had me crossing the sea of black and white marble towards him.

I stood before the mammoth fireplace, the top ledge of which was at least a metre taller than me, and gazed up at the painting. *I wonder what has happened to make one so beautiful and privileged so melancholy,* I thought. I was startled from my thoughts by something moving in my peripheral vision. I braced myself and spun round to behold not the Beast but a silver salver floating in mid-air! I drew breath and, having taken a step back, saw that it held a writing pad. A pen appeared from nowhere, as though pulled from an invisible breast pocket, and began to scratch out the following words on the pad, 'Please do not be alarmed, Miss.'

"If, if you say so …" I said, leaning a little to read them.

The words 'I'm to show you to your quarters, Madam' were scratched out below the others.

"Are … are you the *Beast*?" I asked.

'Goodness me no. I'm the butler, Ashcroft.'

I felt myself taking a step back. "Are you a *ghost*?"

'I do not believe so, Madam. However, I have been this way for so long it's difficult to tell.'

"What way?" I breathed. The pen hovered thoughtfully for a moment before writing 'Without form or speech, Madam.'

"How *horrid* …" I said, glancing up at the portrait of the beautiful young man. "What has happened here? Is this your Master?"

'He was, once upon a time, before …'

"The *Beast*?"

'What keen instincts you possess, Madam.'

"Did … well, did the Beast *kill* him?"

'I fear I have written too much already. Any further questions must be for the Master, Madam.'

I glanced nervously around. "And where *is* your Master?"

'I've little doubt that he will make himself known soon enough. And now, if you would kindly follow me, I will lead to your room.' I followed the silver salver, now lying flat against what I assumed to be the outside of Ashcroft's right leg, up the grand staircase.

At the landing above, it floated down several corridors where paintings and furniture of the finest quality lined every wall. We approached the end of one such corridor where a set of double doors opened as though by magic. As we passed through them into a bedroom, the following question left my lips with a tremble, "Presumably … you are not the only servant here?"

The salver hovered the right side up, and the following was written on the pad: 'No, Madam, I'm not. The palace requires a staff of one hundred to keep it pristine.'

"And are all the servants invisible like you?"

'Yes. You will neither see nor hear any of us.'

"So, I assume that someone just opened the doors?" I said, glancing around the room that contained a four-poster bed, a wardrobe of dark mahogany, and a dressing table.

'You assume correctly, Madam,' wrote Ashcroft. 'Although, I am the only servant to whom the master has given his permission to communicate with you. Your attendant maid has been forbidden to do so.'

"Then, how am I to communicate my needs?" I asked, glancing towards the door.

'Just speak them aloud, Madam. Your attendant maid has ears.'

"And does she also have a name?"

'Her name is Molly. And now, if that is all, I have duties to attend to. I will return shortly to escort you to the dining room where dinner will be served at 7pm.'

"I see, and … will your master be joining me?"

'We have instructions to prepare dinner for *two,* Madam.' I watched the salver float through the door and then noticed my pale and startled reflection in the dressing table's mirror. Feeling exhausted, I stepped towards the four-poster bed that, although fit for a princess, had a hideous gargoyle carved into its headrest. I stopped in my tracks. "*Please* tell me this carving is not an image of your master? How rude of me," I said, approaching the dressing table in search of writing materials. I sat down on the stool and opened the top drawer. Inside was a hairbrush and mirror. I slid the drawer closed and opened the one below it … "A diamond tiara and matching necklace? My sisters would be impressed …" I murmured, sliding the drawer closed. The contents of the third drawer brought a smile to my lips. I lifted out the small writing bureau within and placed it on the dressing table. Inside was a writing pad, inkwell, and pen. I picked up the pen, dipped it in the well and swivelled round to face into the room. "I hope that we shall become friends, Molly. You see, I have been told that I am a captive here, and without at least *one* friend, I fear my captivity will be unbearable. Of course, that's only supposing that your master does not devour me at supper. Anyway," I said with a shudder, "my father came here recently, maybe you saw him?" I held out the pen for her to take. Half a minute passed, and it remained in my hand. "Molly," I said, steeling myself, "I am not as confident or brave as I seem. You see, Father brought me up to always put a brave face on things. I may never see him nor *any* of my family again. So, I'm endeavouring to remember all he taught me for fear of falling apart." Tears filled my eyes, and I felt the pen being drawn from my fingers. I breathed a sigh of relief as the words 'Please don't be afraid. The master would NEVER eat you' were scratched out on the pad.

"Thank you, Molly. That's good to know."

Again, the pen began to write, 'I did see your father. We all did. Our first visitor for a very long time. He caused quite a stir.'

"My father spoke very highly of the hospitality you provided him."

'Thank you, Miss.'

"Please, call me Beauty. It's the name my parents gave me. I'm not big-headed."

'It suits you.'

"Thank you, Molly. If only I could see you, I'm sure I would find that it suited you too. If I may be so bold, what has happened to render you invisible and dumb?"

39

The following words were scratched slowly on the pad, 'You don't *know*?'

I shook my head. "The only thing I know about this palace is that somewhere within it, there lurks a Beast who would only spare my father's life if I took his place. Did ... well, did the Beast do this to you?"

'Oh no, Miss! We have *all* been cursed here. Including the master.'

"Cursed? By who?"

'That is for the master to say.'

"Then I shall ask him."

'Please don't say it was me who put the notion of a curse in your head. I would get into ever so much trouble.'

"You have my solemn promise that no one will ever know of our conversations."

'Thank you.'

"Are all the other servants here as lovely as you?"

'We do our best. Mr Ashcroft is oft to point out that being trapped here for eternity with only each other for company will *feel like* an eternity if we don't get along.'

"Mr Ashcroft is very wise."

'So he likes to tell us. And now we should begin your preparations for dinner, Miss, I mean, Beauty.'

"Preparations? …" As soon as the word left my lips, the pen and pad floated down upon the dressing table. Its top drawer opened, and the brush inside rose into the air. The brush hovered close to the side of my head for a moment before pulling itself gently through my hair. "Thank you, Molly," I sighed, "I have always found having my hair combed soothing …"

Once my hair had been brushed, a power puff floated from the back of the same drawer, and my pale cheeks were given a rosy glow. The power puff floated back inside the drawer, and a moment later, the wardrobe doors opened. I swivelled on my stool to see a ball gown float out of it. It was black and red, strapless and made of the finest silk and taffeta I had ever seen. Quite simply, it was fit for a princess. "It's *lovely* …" I breathed. I stood up and stepped towards the gown that hovered before me. "I have only ever known one set of clothes … which is why my friend Betty and I … although we should obviously *never* discuss such things, considered the possibility that I was an important character. *Particularly* when you consider that my name is not only impossible to live up to but also doubles as a sweeping statement …"

The gown floated down upon the bed, and the pen and pad floated into the air. 'It seems the time has come for another dress is to be part of your story' was written upon it.

I reached down to feel its red silken sleeve. "Apparently so …"

Soon after, I was standing before the full-length mirror in my room, wearing the gown. "… It feels odd, *so much* heavier than the dress I'm used to but …" I heard the scratching of pen on paper and, in my peripheral vision, saw the paper floating towards me. 'You look beautiful in it!' it read.

"Thank you, Molly." A tap on the door startled her, and the pen and pad flew towards the dressing table where they landed with a clink and a clunk. "Have no fear, your secret is safe with me," I whispered before calling "Come in!" The doors opened, and the silver salver hovered into the room and then beckoned to me. I nodded, followed it out into the corridor and stepped cautiously towards my date with destiny.

Journal entry no. 7

Much of that walk behind the floating salver is a blur to me now. Despite the reassurances from Molly that the Beast would not devour me, I could not help but wonder if the lovely girl had only been trying to quell my fears. And Father's report of the Beast had been very different. Indeed, its behaviour had been so fearsome that he would have promised it *anything* to spare his life. And that anything turned out to be me. The only saving grace of this whole situation? I would not wish the apprehension that I felt during that walk upon anyone. I had promised Father that I would attempt to reason with the Beast, but as the doors to the dining room began to open, I wondered if such a thing were possible. *Reason may be beyond this creature!* I thought as I lay eyes upon it for the first time. The Beast was seated at the head of a dining room table and looked so bulky, squat and lumpen that I wondered how its throne-like chair had not buckled and collapsed. Its features were obscured not only by the shadows cast by the fire that crackled behind it but also by the thick fur that covered its face. I dug deep for the strength I needed to walk *towards* the table, but halfway there, I stopped in my tracks, quite unable to move. The Beast rose slowly from its chair and to a height beyond that which *any* living creature that stands upon two legs has a right. I felt so tiny. So frail. So … mortal. The Beast must have sensed this, for its first words were clearly an attempt to reassure me. And reassure me, they might—had its voice, unnaturally deep and monotone, not reminded me of a predatory lion. "Please, come closer; you have nothing to fear from me," it said.

The confident sound of my own voice, once summoned, surprised me. "Nothing to fear? Am I not your prisoner, sir?"

"You are my guest."

"Guest? I did not come here by *choice*."

"Someone made you come? Show me this brute, and I WILL …"

"You will what!?" I gasped.

The Beast's eyes, yellow-tinged and reflective like those of a cat, skirted nervously about the room as though in search of words. "It may be true," it began, "that your father was given the impression that his life was in danger if … if you did not take his place."

"*May* be true?" I replied, and feeling my blood rise, I took several steps forwards and stood behind a chair that had been pulled out. "Did or did you not *force* my father into this odious bargain?"

"I suppose I did. In a manner of speaking."

"There was no *manner of speaking* about it!" At such close quarters, no more than four metres, I imagined that I saw the hint of a smile on that face that, like the face of any beast, has not the capacity to show emotion. The Beast sat slowly, I think so as not to startle me with any sudden movement, and placed its great paws upon the table. Even seated, it was a head taller than me.

I raised my chin. "I have said something that amuses you?"

"To be honest, I was not in the best of moods when I witnessed your father picking that rose."

"You can say that again."

"Are you to stand throughout? Please sit," it said, indicating the chair before me with a wave of its paw.

I sat in the chair that moved forwards and placed me closer to the table. A crystal jug rose into the air and poured some water into my glass. "An invisible servant?" I asked.

"Ashcroft," replied the Beast.

"Thank you, Mr Ashcroft." I fixed the Beast with my most determined gaze. "You were saying that you weren't in the best of moods when you met my father? The fact is, you *terrified* him."

The Beast shrugged. "I can't help how I look."

"None of us can. But you did not have to threaten his life!"

"Really, there is no need for melodrama."

"Melodrama!"

The Beast shuffled uncomfortably in its chair. "Having received word of your father's approach, I instructed the servants to prepare a fire and some food for him. As you are doubtless aware, he fed and warmed himself before falling asleep on a couch."

"You would begrudge your visitor a nap?"

"No, I would not. But then, after all my hospitality, he saw fit to steal from me."

"But it was a *flower*."

"With the benefit of hindsight, I suppose I may have overreacted a little."

"A *little*? Far be it from me to contradict you, but what you did was unforgivable."

"Well then, maybe in time you will find it in your heart *to* forgive me."

"And you imagine that keeping me captive is the way to go about that?"

"Would you stay otherwise?"

"Of course not."

"Then you have your answer. And since I am responsible for you during your 'captivity,' I suggest we eat."

Several silver trays floated into the dining room, and having been placed upon the table, a helping from each was transferred to our plates. "Is it Christmas?" I murmured, looking down at the slices of steaming turkey, roast potatoes, sprouts, and chestnuts. A harpsichord up on a balcony began to play a melancholy tune, and like everyone except for the Beast, its pianist was invisible. This was something I lamented as I observed its table manners. They were ravenous in the extreme and did little to enhance my own appetite. Once it had fed, it picked up a tankard of wine and managed to pour *most* of it down its throat.

"That's disgusting," I barely murmured. The Beast wiped the wine and meat from its chin with a sleeve. It stood up and looked suddenly awkward, perhaps even a little shy. "I … I can only apologise if my table manners have displeased you."

"This is your palace, sir, and you may dine anyway you choose."

The Beast shook its head miserably. "It's time I took my leave. You will dine with me tomorrow evening."

"That didn't sound like a question," I pointed out.

"Indeed, it was not," replied the beast, moving away from the table towards a spiralling staircase at the back of the room.

"So, I *am* your prisoner here?" I called after it.

The beast stopped in its tracks and, over its shoulder, growled, "A bargain is a bargain."

"I'll take that as a yes, then," I murmured as I watched it disappear up the staircase.

Journal entry no. 8

When I returned to my room, my anxiety at being harmed (or even devoured) by the Beast had been replaced by curiosity. Notwithstanding his table manners—after all, he *is* a Beast— he clearly possessed empathy and, dare I think it, reason. I am, therefore, resolved to stop referring to the Beast as 'it.' So, where did *he* come from? Where are the rest of his family? Do they resemble him? And the biggest question of all: how could a creature who resides in such a grand palace not be known throughout the land? I was loathed to ask Molly these questions and compromise her further. After all, she had already told me about the curse. Something I was resolved to ask the Beast about at our next meeting. I lay my head down upon my pillow and said, "Thank you, Molly. For your words of reassurance about your master. Having met him, I no longer consider his eating me a possibility. In truth, I feel rather silly for even considering such a thing. After all, he is the master of his own palace. Not some monster roaming free in a forest."

The pen began to scratch out some words on a sheet of paper on the dressing table. It wafted over to me. 'I'm so pleased!' it read.

"That makes two of us."

'Will there be anything else?'

"No. I'm very tired. I expect you are too. Night night, Molly." I nuzzled my pillow, the softest I had ever placed my head upon, and fell into the most curious sleep.

You might imagine that I had a nightmare about being pursued by a beast, but nothing could be further from the truth. I found myself in a wood, and far from being pursued, *I* was pursuing the young man whose portrait I had so admired when I arrived. He was some way away and staggering from side to side as though injured.

"Wait! Please wait!" I called out. The next I knew, I was standing on one side of a brook, and the young man was observing me, wide-eyed and *fiercely* curious from the other. All I could think was how his portrait, so beautiful and captivating, barely did him justice. Indeed, his dark and brooding eyes possessed a sorrowful longing that stole my breath away. He was panting hard, a hand pressed against his side to relieve a stitch, and clearly nervous of *something* in those woods. He looked so vulnerable that when he suddenly asked, in an off-hand manner, "What are you doing here?" it caught me completely off guard. "What's the matter? Are you lost?" he added.

"Lost? No … I imagined I was dreaming."

The young man looked momentarily puzzled. "Before you say anything more, you should know that a terrible witch lurks in these woods."

"Is that who you were running from?"

He nodded emphatically. "Do I know you?" he asked.

I shook my head. "I have seen you in a portrait."

"Where?"

"In the Beast's palace."

"The *Beast*?" The very mention of the Beast seemed to set the cat amongst the pigeons in his mind; he stumbled but caught himself.

"You must know him," I said.

The young man's eyes opened wide. "*Know him*?"

"Yes. Your portrait hangs in his palace."

"Forgive me. My memory; it plays tricks on me … you must ask the *Beast* … ask him if he knows me."

"I shall."

"She's close … I … I must find cover and hide …" he stammered, stepping backwards away from me.

"But … how will I find you again?"

"Look for me in your dreams!" he shouted with such urgency that I woke with a start. I threw off my covers and climbed out of bed. A candle burned in a silver holder on my dressing table. I picked it up and, stealing my courage, opened my bedroom door and ventured out into the corridor. I hurried as fast as the light from the candle permitted, my bare feet padding on the carpet, my nightdress billowing around me. A minute later, I was descending the main staircase; my destination—the young man's portrait that hung above the fireplace.

I held up my candle, and its flickering light fell onto the face of the young man I had just spoken to. "It *was* you …" I murmured.

Five minutes later, I was wandering through room after room of the palace, in search of someone or something that might explain my dream. I didn't come upon a soul, at least not a visible one, until I pushed open a heavy door and found myself on the upstairs landing of a library. It was the most magnificent library I had ever seen! And the sight of so many volumes stole my breath away. Having stepped forwards and grabbed a handrail, I looked down to behold the Beast. He was sitting in an armchair before a roaring fire, utterly engrossed in a book. The sight of such a large and awkward creature attempting, ever so gently, to turn a page with his claws and not damage it touched my heart. Indeed, such was his interest that he had no idea he was being watched. Even though I had so many burning questions about the young man, the Beast looked so content that I felt loathed to disturb him. I backed slowly from the library and retraced my steps back to my room, intent on asking the Beast *all* my questions at dinner that evening.

Journal entry no. 9

I returned to my bed and slept surprisingly well. When I awoke, I glanced at my bedside table where, had I been at home, the book I was reading would have been waiting. The disappointment at seeing no book was quickly replaced by my recollection of the library. I swept away my bed sheets, jumped out of bed, changed from my nightclothes into my dress and hurried to the door. As soon as I opened it, the aroma of freshly cooked food climbed my nostrils. I looked down to where a silver breakfast tray had been left outside. Upon the tray was a loaf of freshly baked bread, a plate of scrambled eggs, and a glass of orange juice. My stomach rumbled as I stooped to pick up the tray. "Thank you!" I said just in case an invisible servant was close by. My breakfast went down surprisingly well, and as I dabbed at my mouth with a white napkin, a sense of adventure rose in my breast. The prospect of exploring that marvellous library and later quizzing the beast about the young man in my dreams who, for all intents and purposes, felt as though he *was* the man of my dreams filled me with wonder.

My sense of direction must be better than I imagined, for I retraced my steps through that labyrinth of rooms and found myself on the same upstairs balcony in the library. The fire had burned down to its embers, and the armchair where the Beast had sat reading was empty. I hurried down a spiral staircase to my right and, having reached the ground floor, darted into the centre of the library where I spun round to take it all in. I stopped suddenly and placed a hand on the back of the Beast's chair. "Could so many books even be *read* by one person in a single lifetime?" I sighed and, glancing down, noticed that the Beast had left his book on the chair. I picked it up and read the title, *The Golden Ass* by Apuleius. In the sleeve, it was described as 'The story of the overcoming of the impossible obstacles that stood between the love of Psyche and Cupid.' My heart sank at the notion that a beast, as terrifying and ugly as he, might possess a romantic soul. I must admit that at that moment, and even though I was his captive, I felt a pang of pity for him. I was distracted by movement in the corner of my eye. I glanced to my left where a feather duster was cleaning the shelves. I placed the book back down on the chair and made my way over to it.

"Hello," I said to the duster. I cast my gaze about for something the servant might communicate with. I spotted a row of writing desks along the wall to my left. "One moment …" I said, walking over and retrieving a pad and pencil from one.

"I know what you're thinking," I told the duster now hovering at waist height. "That you're not supposed to talk to me. That only Mr Hobbs is afforded that 'privilege.'" I rolled my eyes, lowered my voice and said, "The truth is, and without naming any names, that I've already made one friend since I arrived here. His or her secret is safe with me as yours will be when you write your name on this pad," I said, thrusting the pencil and pad towards the feather duster. Much to my relief, it flew away towards the writing desks as though tossed there in an attitude of wild abandon. It landed beside another pad and pencil, and the following words were scratched out upon it. 'Molly is my best friend, and she has already confided her secret to me! My name is Daphne.'

"It's nice to meet you, Daphne. Do you have to dust *all* these books?"

'Yes. It takes a week to get through them all.'

"It's a fine pastime. I think books are the most magical things. And this collection is surely without equal."

'The master has told me as much many times.'

"Does he come here and read often?"

'This is where he has passed his nights ever since …'

"Since?"

The pencil waggled itself as if to say she could or must not say.

Not wanting to put Daphne in a more awkward position than she already found herself, I changed the subject. "Doesn't your master ever sleep?"

'Only by day.'

I cast my gaze towards the books that Daphne had just finished dusting. "Do you think he'd mind if I borrowed one? If I promise to return it?"

The pen hovered over the pad and scratched out: 'All your needs are to be catered for, just as though you were the mistress of this palace. So help yourself.'

"Your Master told you that?"

'Yes. He visited us in the servant's quarters at dawn, just before he retired to his chamber.'

"A mistress who is also a *prisoner*? What do you know of the whereabouts of the young man in the portrait over the fireplace in the entrance hall?" I asked, sliding a book from a shelf.

'You should only ask such questions of the master.'

"I intend to do just that. I must confess, Daphne, the hours that must pass between now and then cannot pass quickly enough," I said, hugging the book close.

Journal entry no. 10

As she had done the previous evening, Molly helped me change into my gown for dinner. Her fears at breaking the rule that only Hobbs could communicate with me seemed a distant memory, as she scratched her dainty writing across a *great many* sheets of paper. She told me how she'd confided in Daphne, and how excited all the staff were at the prospect of my asking their master about the curse and about the fate of the young man in the portrait. When I told Molly that I'd spoken to him in a dream, it increased her excitement manifold and left her chomping at the bit to share the news with the rest of the household.

When I entered the dining room this evening, the Beast was seated in his chair at the head of the table. Once again, he stood as I approached, and I detected a slight bow of his head. My imagination may have been working overtime, but once I'd reached the table and accepted his gesture to sit, he looked rather nervous. Ever conscious of his bulk, the Beast lowered himself carefully into his seat. "Your room is to your liking? You slept well?" he asked.

"Yes, thank you. My room is … well, it's a most luxurious prison cell."

The Beast cast his gaze down upon the table. "I am sorry you feel that way."

His apology was so heartfelt that I felt compelled to pay him a compliment or, at the very least, say something positive. "I discovered your library this morning ..." I said quietly.

"My library? Was it to your liking?"

"Very much so. How could someone with a love of books such as mine not think it the most extraordinary place? How did you come to own such a collection?"

"The books were collected by many generations of my ..."

"Your *family*?"

The Beast nodded.

I placed my arms on the rests of the chair and, leaning forwards in my seat, said, "I hope you don't think my observation rude, but there are a *great many* portraits in your palace and, well, none of the sitters bear any resemblance to you."

"Just as well," he sighed.

"Why do you say so?"

The Beast looked at me as though he couldn't believe his ears. "If the sitters resembled me, this would be a house of horrors."

"I wouldn't go as far as to say *that* but ..."

"Speak your mind."

"It's just that ... all the servants are invisible and dumb, and their master ..."

"Is a hideous beast?"

"I was about to say is so *melancholy*." I placed my arms upon the table and interlinked my fingers. "I have come here tonight intent on asking you the *two* burning questions ..."

In a mirror image of my own pose, the Beast placed his great arms upon the table and interlinked his claws. He gazed down at them for a moment and then, having raised his sad eyes to meet my own, said, "This has been a palace of secrets for far too long. You have my word that I will answer you *anything* I can."

"Well then ... what has happened here to bring about such sorrow?"

"We have been *cursed*," sighed the Beast, lowering his shoulders as though sharing this burden had relieved them of considerable weight.

"*Cursed*?" I replied, seemingly surprised by this revelation. "By who?"

"A witch. Of the type known to bestow curses throughout this land."

"And when did this unfortunate event occur?"

"Long ago ..."

"And why did she curse you all?"

"Why is something I shall never forget. Not a day has passed between then and now that I have not regretted my actions that night."

I braced myself for the dreaded tale, my imagination conjuring all manner of terrible deeds perpetrated by the Beast upon the witch.

"Believe it or not," sighed the beast, "this palace was once a place of fun and optimism. The parties thrown here were famed throughout the land. So *much* laughter and dancing …"

"I have heard no such tales. In fact, I had no idea this palace even existed before Father told me about it. And he only came upon it by accident. So, how long ago are you talking about?"

"We have been in this wretched state, unknown to the world beyond our gates, for *many* generations."

"But why unknown? Was that part of the curse?"

The Beast nodded. "The night the witch darkened our door, a great storm raged. We have not known its like before or since."

"And did she arrive during one of your parties?"

The Beast shook his head, and I detected the semblance of a smile behind his lion-like features. "The night before had been one of great celebration. Sometimes, when I sit here, I fancy that I can still hear the laughter from that night. The clinking of glasses making toasts to happy futures, the melody played by the fifty-piece orchestra …" said the Beast, closing his eyes and tapping on the table with his claws.

"It sounds like a wonderful party," I said quietly.

The Beast stopped tapping and opened his eyes. "But like all parties, it came to an end. The following morning, as the lightning and thunder raged outside, and the servants were engaged in cleaning, a banging was heard at the front door. Hobbs opened the door and beheld the most wretched of crones, her hair rancid and matted—so long that it hung about her ankles. The creature's back was bent, and she clung to a staff for dear life; its top carved into the shape of a human skull."

"She sounds terrifying …"

"All the more so for the lightning that lit up the sky behind her."

"What did she want?"

Tears welled in the Beast's eyes; he drew a deep breath and said, "Shelter."

I sat back in my chair. "I don't think I'm going to like what's coming next. Hobbs refused her?"

"It is at least some comfort that he did not. I would not have heaped the guilt for what happened next on his shoulders for all the world."

"It was *you* who refused to offer her shelter from the storm?"

The Beast nodded. "Hobbs sent for me. I arrived to discover that she'd jammed her staff in the door and thrust her head and shoulders inside. As I descended the staircase, she must have recognised me as the master. 'Please! I wish only to come inside until the storm has passed," she pleaded. "Dry my clothes before a fire! Drink a cup of hot soup!'"

I cleared my throat uncertainly. "Her requests … they hardly sounded unreasonable."

"Indeed, they were not. But her appearance was such that the servants had shrunk back in horror. As I reached the bottom of the stairs, I heard whispers of evil witches, infectious plagues and worse besides. Believe me when I say she *looked* plague-ridden. Oddly, I can still remember the sight of her bare feet … gnarled black toes with four-inch nails that scraped upon the ground. I was young and hot-headed, and decided I could not risk allowing her entry."

I sighed. "I fear that was not the end of it."

"Your fear is well founded. I told her to leave and never to darken my door again. But far from retreating, she burst through the door and sent Hobbs careering onto his back. She held up her staff as though about to channel a thunderbolt through it. 'Will not one amongst you take pity on a poor old woman?' she cried, her face contorted with rage. Her wretched plea only served to make the servants shrink back further. I glanced about at their frightened expressions, their shaking heads, and again told her to leave my house or risk violence at my hand."

"You threatened her?"

The Beast nodded. "And have regretted doing so from that day to this. That is when she gazed daggers at … at …"

"At *who*?"

"At … at the *portrait* of the young man that hangs above the fireplace. He's … he's my brother … a Prince," stammered the Beast.

"Your *brother*?"

The Beast looked away and nodded. "Somehow the witch knew who he was and said she would place a curse on him to spite me."

"How odd she knew that the Prince was your brother. He's so …"

"Handsome? While I am a beast?"

I shrugged regretfully.

"There is no need to feel guilty about the comparison. The possession of eyes is hardly a crime."

"So, where was your brother at the time?"

The Beast cast his gaze about fretfully. "He … he was elsewhere in the palace … perhaps in the library, for he loved books."

"And the spell, well, did it end his life?" I said, my heart thumping with apprehension at the coming answer.

"No, she did not kill him," murmured the Beast, "rather she *banished* him to endure a lifetime of loneliness. And told me that I would never gaze upon his face again."

"And you haven't seen him since?"

The Beast raised a paw and gripped his face as though it were a mask he could pull away. He lowered his hand slowly and said, "I have not laid eyes upon him from that day to this."

"And have you never thought to look for him? After all, the witch must have banished him *somewhere*."

"Look for him?" said the Beast, his eyes flashing up to meet my own. "If only it were that simple."

"Have you not at least tried?"

The Beast seemed unsure of how to answer my question. "… My appearance, it prevents me from venturing beyond the palace grounds. People fear that which they do not understand. I would be set upon by angry mobs, seen as a monster."

"It's true … people can be so cruel."

The Beast sat back in his chair. "After she cast her spell upon my brother, she turned her rage upon my servants, informing them that from that moment on, they would mirror their stations in life and become invisible and silent, never to be seen nor heard again." The Beast clenched his fists. "I have neither seen nor heard them since that day. Indeed, your father was the first person I had seen in years."

I felt the hairs on the back of my neck stand on end. "You must have been *so* lonely."

"Doubtless the very punishment the witch had in mind."

I sat back in my chair and, having ordered my thoughts, said, "Ever since seeing your brother's portrait, I have found myself …"

The Beast leaned forwards, most attentively, in his chair.

"That's to say," I went on, "I have seen something in your brother's face that has quite arrested me and …"

"And?"

"I had a dream about him …" I glanced at the Beast whose expression was so hungry that it compelled me to go on. "In the dream, I found and spoke to your brother, and most bizarrely, it felt as though I was the only person who *could*."

The Beast sat back in his chair, and his eyes filled with a longing to tell me something that he was either unwilling or unable to. It was then that I heard myself utter, "I … *we* must find the Prince together and rescue him."

The Beast's eyes opened wide. "*Rescue?*"

I nodded.

He clambered to his feet, turned his back to me and said, "But that is surely impossible …"

I jumped up, walked the length of the table and placed a hand upon his shoulder. "I beg to differ, for, in a land such as this, *anything* is possible."

The Beast looked at my hand on his shoulder. "Maybe, within reason," he said quietly.

"What's more, we must right *all* the wrongs that have happened here."

"And how do you suggest we do that? Where even to start?"

"With the witch that cast the spell in the first place. If *anyone* knows where your brother has been banished, it is her."

The Beast turned to face me. "You're suggesting we find the witch?"

"Yes! You said so yourself; she was old and carried a staff. How far can she have travelled?"

"Far indeed if she turned her staff into a broomstick and took flight."

"We must at least *try* to think positive."

"Maybe I have forgotten how."

"Then I shall remind you."

"Even if we found her, why do you imagine she would … that she'd give us any clues as to where to find my brother?"

"All I know is that if we don't try, we shall never know. Surely, it's a chance worth taking. And we might also discover a way to free the servants from the curse." As I finished speaking, a jug of water that had been floating in the air fell and smashed upon the ground.

"Hobbs …" sighed the beast with a shake of his head. A writing pad and pen appeared and hovered over the broken jug. We both watched as these words were hurriedly scratched upon it. 'Please listen to our visitor, Master! We've waited so long for someone to bring us hope.'

The Beast looked at me. "I will need time to think …"

"All right. But I, we'll expect your answer tomorrow night. Won't we, Mr Hobbs?"

'Indeed, we shall, Madam.'

Journal entry no. 11

After dinner, I returned to my room, my mind alive at the prospect of lifting the curse and of rescuing the young Prince who, although I had never met outside of a dream, now occupied my every waking thought.

So, when at last I fell asleep and found myself returned to the same woods as before, I could not have been happier. I gazed about for sight of the Prince but could see nothing but trees and blue skies. "Hello?" I called. "I have such hopeful news. *Please* reveal yourself."

There was no reply.

"But you *must* be here. Why else would I have been returned?"

"Your optimism becomes you ..." came the voice of the Prince from behind me. I spun around with hungry eyes but saw no one. "Where ... where are you?" I breathed.

"Less than a metre away ... standing right in front of you."

"Admittedly, you sound very close, but ... I can't see you."

"Then please, you *must* try harder."

"Try harder?" I said, going at first boss and then bug-eyed.

"No!" blurted the Prince.

"Sorry. But how else am I to try harder to see?"

"Clearly … well, clearly it is not enough to look for me with your eyes alone," said the prince, sounding increasingly alarmed.

"All right. But to my knowledge, I possess nothing else that enables me to see."

"Of *course* you do."

I placed my hands upon my hips. "Well?"

"Your extraordinary heart."

"Oh, I see. Or rather, I still don't," I said, lowering my hands.

"Close your eyes," said the Prince gently

"Okay …"

"Good. Now cast your mind back to the first time you laid eyes upon my portrait …"

"Okay, yes, I see it, in my mind's eye …"

"Now tell me, what did you feel in that instant?"

Talk about fishing, I thought. "I felt … well, I felt a deep connection to something, to *someone* …"

"To see me, you need only focus on that connection again, and then open your eyes."

I opened my eyes and beheld the Prince standing before me, his expression so grave that I felt compelled to reach out and place a palm upon his cheek. "… I see you now."

"I am more relieved than you can imagine," he replied, his eyes searching my own as though for a glimpse of his own reflection. "And I see you …"

"And, I'm not a disappointment?" I asked, shamelessly fishing for a compliment of my own.

The Prince smiled. "How could a person capable of seeing beyond my appearance to the person beneath *ever* be a disappointment?"

I laughed nervously. "But you are *handsome*. So why assume such things about me?"

The Prince took a moment to consider his reply. "Believe me when I tell you," he began, having chosen his words carefully, "that the nature of the curse is such that only a person of considerable empathy, kindness and strength could *ever* see me."

"I thank you for your kind words and have some of my own to tell you."

"You bring news, then?"

"The very best! I have spoken to your brother and have all but convinced him that we must rescue you. To this end, we will seek the witch who banished you here."

"But … would not such a quest be exceedingly dangerous?"

"Yes, but you know what they say: 'Nothing ventured, nothing gained,'" I replied, making light of my fears.

"Then you should know that the witch is as fearsome as she is cruel," said the Prince, casting his gaze about, "so, your own banishment, or *worse*, may be gained."

"None-the-less," I said, standing just about as tall as I could, "we will find and, if necessary, *plead* with her for some clue as to how the curse may be broken."

The Prince ran a shaky hand through his hair. "You would really take such a risk for me?"

"Not just you. The servants have suffered greatly as has your poor brother. Surely, you have all suffered long enough. More than paid your price for not providing the witch sanctuary that night."

The Prince nodded. "You will get no argument from me. And my brother has agreed that the time has come to make such an approach?"

I shrugged. "He's going to give me his decision at our meeting tomorrow."

The Prince sighed. "I'm sorry that you should have to negotiate with a creature of such loathsome appearance."

"Nonsense! I should not have to explain to you of *all* people the importance of looking beyond the surface."

"Then, you don't find my brother as loathsome as his beastly nature would suggest?"

"Not at all. Your brother is not in the *least bit* loathsome," I said, feeling oddly protective of him.

"So, you find him, if not friendly, at least courteous?"

"I can assure that beyond luring me to his castle in the first instance, your brother has been as friendly and courteous as it is humanly possible to be."

"*Humanly*? So many years have passed since my brother has had another to converse with he fears he may have lost his humanity."

I placed a hand upon the Prince's muscular shoulder. "It's been so long since you've seen him. How is it that you know your brother's fears so well?"

The Prince blinked some moisture from his eyes. "… Know? I, I don't *know*; I just assumed …"

"Please do not fret …" The prince took my hands in his own, raised them to his lips and then, having kissed them tenderly, opened his eyes urgently. "I … I have been found … she's pulling me back to my confinement!" One moment, I was looking into the Prince's pleading eyes, and the next, I had woken with a start.

I climbed out of bed, put on my dressing gown and picked up the lit candle from my dressing table. I hurried from the room in the direction of the library where I hoped to discover the Beast.

I arrived in the library, upon the usual upstairs balcony, and seeing the Beast stood over a table below, I breathed a sigh of relief. I padded down the spiral staircase, skirted across the floor and arrived at the table.

"What is the meaning of this?" breathed the Beast, clutching at his chest.

"Forgive me, I … I had no wish to startle you but …" My attention had been drawn by the numerous books and maps on the table. "You're planning a journey …" I smiled, and, leaning over the map, I saw that the Beast had written a question mark over an area of caves. As my heart quickened at the possibility of it being the witch's lair, I looked up and met his inquisitive gaze. "I've had another dream about your brother," I said.

The Beast averted his gaze in that way of his that makes me suspicious that he has something to hide. He looked down at the map. "And did you speak with him?" he asked.

"Yes," I said, leaning forwards and attempting to see his dark eyes that might reveal his secret.

"And what did my brother have to say for himself?"

"He was buoyed by the news that we're going to look for him," I said, casting my gaze over the books and maps. "You've been doing some research? *Please* tell me this has something to do with locating the witch?"

The Beast turned, stepped towards the fireplace and looked into its flames. "It does," he murmured.

"And this X," I said, lifting the map from the table, "is it the location of her lair?"

"Your guess is as good as mine," said the Beast quietly.

"Hardly. Not least because you have done all this research. So, is this the location of the witch, or isn't it?"

"It is my best guess."

"So," I pressed, "your mind is made up that the time has come to do something about this curse?"

The Beast returned to the table and surveyed the documents. "I suppose it must be ..."

"So, we leave for the witch's lair tomorrow?"

"Tomorrow?"

"Yes. They say that there is no time like the present."

The Beast placed a claw on the map and traced a line of blue that ran from the location of the cave through the hills and countryside to another location upon a cliff top. "We are here," he pointed out.

I leaned over the map. "Really? I had no idea that your palace was built on a cliff that overlooks a lagoon."

"Why would you? You approached from the front. Now, to journey to the cave my research suggests is where we will discover her lair, we must navigate this river by boat ..."

"You have a boat?"

"I do."

"So, we leave tomorrow, then?"

The Beast shook his head. "As you might imagine, it has been a great many years since anyone has set sail in my boat. And the last time I visited the lagoon, I noted that it needed repair."

"So how long do you think it will take to get the boat ready?"

The Beast shrugged. "A week at the very least."

The Beast's armchair was just behind me, and as I lowered my myself slowly into it, he said, "Something troubles you?"

I perched on the edge of the chair and looked down at my clasped hands. "It's … it's just that this journey may be dangerous and …"

"And you have changed your mind? If you have, then I understand. Indeed, it was presumptuous of me to …"

"What? *No*. Of *course* I haven't changed my mind. It's just that if there's a chance that I may not see my family again, I would very much like to visit them one last time." I looked up at the Beast. "If I promise to return within six days so that we might set off on the seventh, would you allow me to go?"

The Beast placed a paw upon the table as though for support. "Yes, of *course* you should visit your family before embarking upon such a perilous expedition." I raised myself up off the chair, placed my hand on his paw and squeezed it tenderly. "You have my word that I shall return to you on the sixth day." The Beast stared at my hand, so tiny and fragile atop his own, and drew breath …

"Breathe out …" I urged him.

"… You can *bear* to touch such a monstrous … such a monstrous …"

"Of *course*."

"Forgive me, Beauty. It just that it has been so long since I have felt an affectionate gesture that …"

"You feared you might never feel one again?"

The Beast nodded.

Journal entry no. 12

This morning I awoke at dawn, and as I opened my eyes, I remembered the dangerous yet exciting journey the Beast and I were to embark upon in seven days. "Once he has repaired his boat …" I said, drawing back my bed clothes. I sat up and smiled at the recollection that I was to see my family that very day. The thought of surprising my father and Betty filled my heart with joy. As I leapt out of bed and reached for my dress, I heard the scratching of a nib on paper. "Molly? Is that you?" I said, casting my gaze about. "I very much hope it *is*," I continued as I slid into my dress.

'Of course, it's me' was written above the words she had already written, which were: 'A coach has been made ready to take you home.'

"I am to return home today, yes!" I said, securing the belt about my waist which, as is generally the case with fairytale characters, must be pulled *ridiculously* tight to reach its single fastening.

'PLEASE say you shall return! All the servants are so worried that you're not going to,' Molly scratched on the pad.

"That's very sweet of everyone. Please reassure them that I have every intention of returning …"

'When?'

"In just six days' …" I said, sitting on the edge of the bed and pulling on my shoes.

'Do you promise?'

"I do," I said, standing. "In one week, your master and I are to embark upon an adventure …" I crossed to the dressing table and sat down. I picked up the brush but felt it pulled gently from my fingers. As Molly began to comb the tangles from my hair, she somehow managed to write with her free hand, 'An adventure to help the master???'

"I hope that its outcome will lessen his guilt and restore his peace of mind, yes. You see, we're to search for the witch that banished his brother and rendered you all invisible."

'And if you find her?'

"*When* we find her, we shall start by asking her how we might atone and put things right."

Molly drew a smiling face on the pad and, under it, wrote: 'THANK YOU! But be careful. She's dangerous.'

I nodded. "But your master seems very resourceful and … I feel strangely comforted by the idea of being accompanied by him."

Molly drew another smiling face on the pad, this one considerably larger than the first.

The carriage that awaited outside was larger and grander than my previous conveyance, and being aware of at least *some* of the palace's secrets now, I realised that the horses (there were four of them) were not blessed with a remarkable sense of direction at all. "There must be an invisible coachman," I murmured.

As I was about to climb inside, I turned and looked up at the palace, half expecting to see the Beast watching me from some high up window. Seeing no one, I drew a deep breath, climbed aboard and, no sooner had I taken my seat, then the carriage moved away. The carriage's opulent interior, with its gold fixtures and fittings, and seats upholstered in red velvet made me feel like a VIP. Across from me was a seat large enough for three adults. "Or one Beast," I murmured, imagining him sitting there and gazing out of the window in that tortured yet knowing way of his. I felt a pang of something that I could not quite put my finger on. Then, as though my imagination had performed a conjuring trick, the Beast's image was replaced by the Prince's. He sat in the middle of the seat, smiling across at me in such a way as to give me goosebumps. These two brothers, so very different in appearance, and yet so similar in other ways, occupied my every thought on that journey home. So much so that when the carriage pulled up outside my family house, it felt as though no time had passed at all. The front door flew open, and Father came through it. He was all smiles and tears, and the moment I stepped down from the carriage, he practically hugged the air from my lungs. He held me at arm's length, looked me over for signs of damage and, seeing none, smiled and hugged me again. "You have returned to us safe and sound! I knew you'd charm the Beast!"

"It's good to see you, Father," I smiled, "but rest assured the Beast is not what you think. Not at all ferocious. Just sad and lonely." I heard footsteps skirting across the pebbled drive and saw Betty rushing towards me. "Beauty!" she cried.

Father took a step back so I might hug my best friend. "The Beast has not devoured you, then!" she cried into my shoulder.

"Of *course,* he hasn't!" I said, hugging her.

"You've escaped?"

"I had no need of escape. And what is more, it's my intention to return to his castle."

"What? You're going *back?*" said Father.

"Indeed, I am. Let's go inside, and I'll tell you all about it." I reached for Betty's hand and gave it a squeeze. "We shall go for a walk later. How I've missed our walks."

"And you'll tell me all your news?"

"Of course!"

The first thing to strike me as I entered my grand family home was just how tiny it felt compared to the palace. In the parlour, my sisters jumped up from a couch where they'd been conversing in hushed tones and welcomed me with forced grins. "What a wonderful surprise!" enthused one.

"Yes, we imagined we might never see you again!" said the other.

"It's so good to see you both," I said with all sincerity. I kissed them on the cheek and looked at Father. "Where are my brothers?"

"Oh, you know your brothers; always away doing this and that," said Father, sitting at the head of the parlour's table. "Take a seat one and all ..." he smiled, "Beauty is going to tell us about her time at the palace."

"She looks very well *considering* ..." said one of my sisters, taking her seat.

"Thank you," I replied, taking my own. "The truth is that reports of the Beast's monstrous nature have been much exaggerated."

Father cleared his throat nervously. "He did threaten my life, Beauty."

I reached across the table and placed my hand on his. "Having spent time with him, I am convinced that he did not mean it."

"And were reports of its hideous appearance *also* exaggerated?" asked a sister.

"Indeed, they were not," shuddered Father.

"Don't refer to him in that way, sister," I said.

"In what *way*?" replied my sister, sounding unjustly reprimanded.

"As an *it*," I said.

"But I don't understand," huffed the other sister, "is *it* a beast, or isn't *it*?"

I drew a deep breath. "His appearance can only have been an accident of birth. Underneath he is most certainly *not* an it. What's more, he is possessed of a kind and noble heart."

"She always has had a soft spot for freaks," giggled one of my sisters to the other.

"That's quite enough of that," Father admonished her.

"Indeed," I went on undeterred, "the Beast's own brother is *very* handsome. And a prince."

My sisters glanced irritably at one another. "And was this handsome prince at the palace?"

I looked down at my hands in my lap.

"Beauty? What's the matter?" asked Father.

"To answer your question, *no*, the Prince was not at the palace. You see, he was banished long ago by a witch's curse." I looked up. "And it's my intention to …" I paused, as sitting there at that table with at least *one* sympathetic face, my resolve at the thought of what the Prince had endured through no fault of his own began to crumble.

"Beauty? What has upset you?" asked Father.

"She looks about ready to burst into tears," observed one of my sisters with a roll of her eyes. "Oh, go on; tell us. What errand of mercy have you got in mind *this* time?" I have always tried to be as patient as possible with my sisters, and at times, they have tested this patience to its limits. This was one such time. "The Prince," I said, glaring back and forth between them, was banished by a witch to endure a lifetime of solitude. He has not been seen since, and it will come as no surprise to either of you that I am intent on finding and rescuing him."

"Rescuing him?" said Father, throwing up his hands.

"Yes, Father. I have spoken with him in my dreams and …"

"In your dreams?" scoffed one of my sisters.

"Yes, but it was *more* than that."

"Our sister can't find a *real* Prince, only a foul Beast, it seems, and so has invented a phantom one," giggled a sister.

"He will no longer be a phantom once I, *we*, his brother and I have rescued him."

"It sounds very dangerous," cautioned Father, "won't the witch have something to say on the matter? I presume the Prince gave her good reason for banishing him."

"No, that's just it. The witch punished the Prince for the deeds of his brother and his servants. You see, it was *they* who refused her sanctuary from a storm."

"Well then, if that's the case, what punishment did the witch inflict upon the *Beast*?" asked Father.

I sighed mournfully. "It seems that his punishment was to live with the guilt of his actions. And what is more, the witch struck his servants invisible and dumb. So, he has been forced to endure a lifetime alone, surrounded by people he can neither see nor hear."

"That explains why I saw no one during my visit," mused Father.

We all sat in silence for a moment, a silence broken by a sudden knock at the door. The door opened, and two gentlemen were shown into the parlour by our footman. My sisters, fawning and preening with every step, hurried over and laid claim to each by seizing an arm. Father and I stood and greeted the young men with a bow. They were army officers with straight backs and long noses which they looked down imperiously. "Welcome back to my home, gentlemen," said Father, "and may I introduce my other daughter, Beauty. Beauty, this is Captain Black and Captain Manners." Their eyes opened wide as they beheld me, and having broken free of my sisters' grasps, they presented themselves to me with a bow. A glance in the direction of my sisters told me it would be best to make myself scarce. Besides, I was positively chomping at the bit to tell Betty about my time at the palace.

Journal entry no. 13

Upstairs, I found Betty pacing back and forth on the landing outside my bedroom.

"I thought I would never see you again!" she cried as she threw her arms around me.

"If I'm honest, I feared the same …"

"I've kept your room *exactly* as it was when you left," she said, reaching for the door handle.

"Thank you …" She opened the door, and we stepped inside.

"You must have missed your room so much, what with being locked in some horrible dungeon?"

I shook my head. "The Beast has been most hospitable."

Betty shrugged in a bitter-sweet way. It suggested that while she would not wish me to suffer, she didn't much like the idea of my preferring the Beast's lodgings. "This will *always* be home," I smiled, and taking her hands in my own, we sat upon my bed.

"So," asked Betty, "is the name of your story to be Beauty and the Beast as you feared?"

I considered her question for a moment. "Beauty and the Beast's *Brother*, perhaps? Oh, Betty! It will sound *so* pathetic, but I was overwhelmed when I first saw his portrait!"

"His portrait? But you have met him?"

"… Yes," I nodded, "in a dream, well, in *two* dreams, actually."

"But never in person?"

"Not yet. But these were not your average dreams. And the Prince's brother, the Beast, thought them so important that he has agreed that we must act on them."

"How?"

"We're to go on an expedition to find the witch who banished him."

"You're intent on finding a *witch*?" Betty gasped.

"We are," I replied with a conviction that surprised me.

"Please, think again! What if she banishes you? I might never see you again."

"At times such as this, we must think of others before ourselves. This isn't about me. The witch cursed *all* the servants at the palace, and unless somebody does *something*, they will be forced to endure an eternity of being invisible and dumb. Molly, my maid and friend at the Palace, can only communicate with me by writing on a pad."

"Cripes. You mean you've never seen her?"

I shook my head.

"That's too weird," shuddered Betty, "like being haunted."

"It's *exactly* like being haunted. A terrible fate for anyone to suffer."

"Poor you," nodded Betty.

"Not me. The servants."

"Oh, I see. So how long are you staying here? Where you can at least *see* who you're talking to."

"I promised I'd return to the castle in six days."

"Six *days*? Is that all?"

"Yes, but we shall make the most of them!"

And make the most of them, we did. At least for the first couple of days, during which time we strolled around town, gossiping and laughing and, once or twice, nimbly avoiding those who were gossiping about me. We stuffed our faces at Mince's Cake Shop, our favourite, and danced in the fountain in the main square. But on the third day, things took a turn for the worse when Father had an accident. It was early in the morning, and I'd been dozing, thinking about you know who, when I was returned from those woods by the sound of shattering glass. I leapt out of bed, rushed from my room, and bolted down the main staircase where Father lay sprawled on his back at the bottom. Several servants had converged on him, and as I reached the bottom of the stairs, they stepped back so I could crouch beside him. I took his limp hand in my own, "Father! Father? Can you hear me?

Quickly!" I continued glancing up at the shocked faces of the servants. "Summon Dr Fine!"

An hour later, Father, still unconscious, had been carried to his bed where, having bandaged his head, Dr Fine was checking his pulse. "He will be okay, won't he, doctor?" I asked. Doctor Fine, a tall, portly man who likes to wear brightly coloured cravats and waistcoats, returned the watch he had used to check Father's pulse to his pocket. "Your papa has suffered a severe knock to his head ..." he said gravely.

"But Father is strong ... he *is* going to wake up, isn't he?"

"Only time will tell ..." sighed the doctor. It was then that my sisters, having recently arrived home from a shopping expedition, entered Father's bedroom. At the sight of him lying prone and with his head bandaged, one clasped her cheeks while the other exclaimed, "What has Beauty *done* to papa?"

I looked over at them. "No one has done anything to him. Father's had an accident ..." I said, returning my tearful gaze to him.

Doctor fine closed his bag. "Ladies," he began quietly, "your papa has suffered a calamitous blow to his head. I have done all I can to make him comfortable." He picked up his medical bag and, addressing us all, said, "The next 48hrs will be crucial. If he doesn't show some sign of waking, then ..."

"So, what should we do?" I asked.

"Stay by his side and *talk* to him," said doctor Fine.

"*Talk* to him," scoffed one of my sisters, "can he hear us?"

"How could he?" said the other. "Just *look* at him. He's dead to the world."

I looked at the doctor imploringly.

"Your father's in a coma. In similar cases, when the patient *has* woken, they have reported that not only were they able to hear the voices of their loved ones, but that they found them a great comfort."

"Then I shall remain by his side and ..." I said, swallowing the lump that had come to my throat.

"You do that," said one of my sisters as though it was the least that I could do.

Through Father's open window, we heard a carriage pull up outside. "Our beaus?" said one of my sisters, glancing at the other.

"They are taking us to lunch. It's all arranged. It would be rude to cancel."

"And we will bring Father back a present, won't we, sister?"

"That's a lovely idea!" said the other, interlinking her arm.

"You two go. I will stay by Father's side ..." I said.

My sisters nodded, turned, and then hurried from the room.

Journal entry no. 14

This is the first time that I've have had the presence of mind to write in my journal for *five* whole days. During that time, I have barely slept, eaten, or left Father's room. On the first day, the day of his accident, I held his hand in my own and spoke fondly of the years gone by. Once or twice, I imagined I saw movement, some flicker of recognition behind his closed eyes.

On the third day, doctor Fine returned to check on Father's progress. He did not say so in as many words, but the graveness of his tone led me to fear that because Father had not woken, it was now doubtful that he ever would. After the doctor left, and finding my troubled mind unable to remember anything else, I decided to read to Father. I brought his favourite books from his study and read them aloud. It was on the fifth day, while midway through a scientific tone about the movement of the planets around the sun, that Father cleared his throat as though trying to speak. I dropped the book and cried, "Father! Dear Father! I am here! Your daughter, Beauty. *Please* wake, Father." Father's eyes opened and, after no little effort, focused on me. "Water …?" he croaked.

"Yes, of course!" I filled a glass from a jug on his bedside table and held it to his parched lips. Father grimaced as he drank, and once he'd had his fill, I put down the glass and ran to the door. "Fetch doctor Fine! Someone fetch the doctor! Father has come back to us!"

"How long have I been unconscious," I heard him ask from behind me.

"Five days. But you are back with us now …"

"You look … so … *pale* Beauty …"

"Please, you mustn't concern yourself with me," I said, returning to my chair by his side.

"And your brothers and sisters?"

"My brothers are yet to return from their trip …"

Father closed his eyes. "And your sisters?"

"Have been *very* worried about you, Father."

"I can remember only hearing your voice, Beauty," he said, reaching for and finding my hand upon his bed.

"That is because I have made a point of making *sure* you heard it. Doctor Fine said that in cases such as yours, the voice of a loved one can help recovery. You must have grown so tired of hearing it."

"Tired? Not for a second," said Father, opening his eyes. "I followed its sound, and it … it led me *back* to this room." Father's brows knitted, and he looked suddenly anxious. "What is it?" I asked him.

"… I have been unconscious for *five* days?"

I nodded. "But you are back now, and that is all that counts."

Father shook his head, and tears filled his eyes. "I don't deserve you …"

"Nonsense."

"It's true. It was because of me that you had to go away. Mercifully, the Beast allowed you to return. But only if you promised him you'd return by the *sixth* day. If I have been unconscious for five, then this must already be the seventh! Which means that you have broken your promise to him."

I sat back in my chair. "I have shut all thoughts of other commitments from my mind. I would not have left you in your unconscious state for all the world. I'm sure the Beast will understand. I hope that he will."

"You must go back to him today! Honour that commitment, my dear. Ever since you returned and told us your story, I have had a good feeling about what fate holds for you. I believe this to be your destiny, Beauty."

"Please, Father, *rest*," I sighed, feeling a dreadful pang of anxiety at having broken my promise to the Beast.

Journal entry no. 15

During the hours that followed, Father made a remarkable recovery. So much so that even gloomy doctor Fine was impressed with what he called his 'robust attitude.' It was certainly true that Father appeared remarkably full of beans for someone who had just emerged from a coma. Although I could tell that such was Father's desire for me to fulfil my destiny, that he was doing his best to appear as well as possible.

To be honest, now Father was on the mend, my worries for him were matched only by my growing anxiety over being a day late for my return to the palace. After all, the Beast was not the most confident of fellows, and although a single day is not so long in the grand scheme of things, to a troubled mind like the Beast's, it may feel a good deal longer. Soon after, reports came from the stable that his horses, the ones that had brought me home, had grown agitated. I visited the stables to find them stomping back and forth in their stalls, desperate to be free. "Please, prepare the horses and carriage for my return to the palace," I implored the stable boys, "I intend to leave within the hour!"

I returned to Father's bedroom and discovered him sitting up in bed and smiling as doctor Fine took his pulse. "I'm going to take your advice, Father, and return to the palace without delay."

"Oh, what splendid news! Just the tonic," replied Father.

Doctor Fine retrieved a stethoscope from his bag. "Are you really so tired of hearing her voice?" he murmured as he pressed the silver disk to Father's chest.

"Goodness me no," said Father with a shake of his head.

"It's okay, Father …" I smiled.

"I shall miss her terribly, Doctor. But Beauty *must* follow her destiny, and it awaits her at the palace …"

"Oh, yes, and what *palace* might that be …" murmured doctor Fine, removing the stethoscope from his ears.

Father and I exchanged a glance.

"It's not in this district," I said, "it's very doubtful you will have heard of it."

"Obviously … there are no palaces in this district," he said, closing his bag. "And now I shall be on my way."

I jumped up. "But you will return *soon* to check on Father, won't you?"

"Have no fear of that. I shall be back the day after tomorrow."

"Thank you, Doctor," I said extending my hand, which he shook.

After the doctor left, and I was saying goodbye to Father, my sisters came into his room. "We hear you're to leave us. To return to your Beast?" said one.

"Yes," I said, smoothing down my dress with the palms of my hands.

"Indeed, it is time," said Father somewhat mysteriously.

"*Time?*" asked my sisters.

"For Beauty to seek her true destiny."

"Well then, let's hope that her *true destiny* isn't to be devoured by a ferocious beast," said one of my sisters.

The other nodded profusely. "How *awful* would that be."

"I have no doubt that that is *not* your sister's destiny," said Father, extending his arms so I might hug him one last time before my departure. "I know in my heart of hearts that you will find your happy ending, Beauty. No one deserves to more than you," he whispered.

"Thank you, Father."

Having said my goodbyes to my family, I searched the house and garden for Betty. My search was in vain. Indeed, no one had seen her all morning. And one of the stable boys reported that she had gone into town on some errand and that she would not return for several hours. So it was that, with a heavy heart, I climbed aboard the carriage, its horses no less agitated, and settled back into the seat. The horses flew away at such speed that I was sent sliding from one end of the bench to the other where, having reached for a leather strap, I clung on for the remainder of the journey.

The castle, when it *finally* hooved into view, appeared more gloomy and troubled than ever. I told myself that it was just my imagination playing tricks on me. But as I climbed out of the carriage, my trepidation had me flying up the steps towards the open door. Once inside, my gaze found the Prince's portrait, and despite my need to find the Beast and lay my fears to rest, I was frozen at the sight of it. "Move, Beauty, move! …" I told myself, and with that, I darted forwards towards the stairs. Ignoring the curious trail of red petals that lay upon them, I continued in the direction of my room where I hoped to find Molly.

Molly was obviously nowhere to be seen, but what could be seen were the words she'd written on my dressing table's mirror in red lipstick: Follow the trail of rose petals to the boathouse!

Diary entry no. 16

I followed the trail of petals back down the stairs as quickly
as my legs would carry me. At the bottom, they snaked
around to a door behind the staircase. The door opened onto
a long gallery; its high walls hung with ornate mirrors. I
followed the red trail down the gallery, my pale and quickly
moving reflection on either side of me, and through a door at
the end into a magnificent ballroom. A grand piano stood
alone and adrift at its centre—so alone that it reminded me of
the Beast. "I *must* find you," I murmured as I followed the
trail of petals across the ballroom and outside onto a veranda.
The view took my breath away: glinting in the light of a full
moon, a great lake was surrounded by mountains. I went to
the edge of the veranda and, grasping the handrail, felt dizzy
as I looked down upon a lagoon where a single ship sat
against a dock. The red trail continued down a flight of steps
to my right, which seemed to descend *forever*. At the bottom,
I ran towards the dock where, for the first time, I could see
that the ship had been badly damaged—its sails torn, its
masts hacked down, and worst of all, smoke from an
extinguished fire hovered above it like a vengeful wraith. I
moved swiftly to the key side and saw the Beast slumped
against some rocks.

"Whatever has happened here!" I cried, glancing towards the wrecked boat. The Beast's eyes opened wide, and a bottle he was holding fell and smashed upon the ground. He clambered uneasily to his feet. "I …" he said, staggering a little.

"Are you hurt? Were you attacked?"

"You *have* returned?"

"Clearly. Are you *drunk*?"

"I was thirsty and …"

I looked towards the ruined ship. "Did you do this?"

The Beast shrugged his shoulders and slumped miserably against the wall for support.

"But why?" I asked. "You were supposed to *fix* it."

"When you did not return, I … I thought that it was no longer needed."

"I'm a *day* late. My father had an accident. I could not leave him until he'd recovered."

"And he is well now?" asked the Beast with as much dignity as one so guilty could muster.

"Yes, he is quite well now. Which is more than can be said for the *ship*."

"So, now you see …" slurred the Beast.

"See?"

"Who or, should I say, *what* you have returned to? I was not just *made* a hideous Beast on the outside, but given a beast's rage within."

"*Made* a beast?" I asked, for it seemed a curious choice of words.

Avoiding my gaze, the Beast replied, "It was … it was just a figure of speech. Born, made, what's the difference?"

I approached him and said calmly, "You cannot help who you are. Just as I cannot help who I am."

"You?" he said, looking down at me, "but you … you are …"

"I believe the words you're looking for are: overly talkative, opinionated and rather annoying."

The Beast shook his head.

"So, what's to be done about a ship? Might you still be able to repair this one?"

The Beast surveyed his savage handiwork. "The damage is too great. Our only hope is to hire one."

"From where?" I asked, looking at the lagoon and mountains that rose high above it.

The Beast took several steps towards the lagoon. "A fishing village lies a day's ride down river …"

"But we have no ship to take us there."

"A lifeboat will serve us well for such a journey," said the Beast, pointing at the little craft suspended at the back of the smouldering ship. Hope had just begun to rise again in my chest when we heard a terrible scream. It was so unexpected, coming as it did from neither the Beast nor myself (the only people for miles around capable of making such a sound) that we both jumped. I spun about, and gazing at the walkway that overlooked us, I saw Betty! She was staring, wide-eyed at the Beast, her hands clasped to her cheeks. My heart sank as the Beast turned away from her as though in shame. "Who ... who is that *person*?" he breathed.

I placed a comforting hand upon his back. "That is my good friend, Betty."

"What's she doing here?"

"I had no idea she *was* here. She must have hidden in the carriage," I said, glancing up to see her cowering in the shadows.

"Go to her," said the Beast, "go to her and tell her that I mean her no harm, that ..."

"That you've already had your supper?"

The Beast looked at me with fondness in his eyes. "That would be a good place to start."

I reached Betty in the nick of time, for as she threw her arms around me, her quivering form collapsed and pulled us both to the ground. "Oh, dear Betty! What on *earth* are you doing here," I said, rolling off her.

Journal entry no. 17

The Beast insisted on carrying Betty back to my room, something I thought very gracious, considering that it had been the sight of him that caused her to faint. Indeed, such was the Beast's determination—to get her there and leave before she awoke—that it was all I could do to keep up with him.

Once back in my room, I could not help but feel touched by the gentleness with which he lay her upon my bed. After doing so, he moved to the door and, over his shoulder, said, "When she wakes, tell her that she is welcome here. That she may stay as long as she wishes."

"Thank you," I replied, sitting on the bed beside her.

"And now, if you'll excuse me, I will make the lifeboat ready for our departure at dawn. That's if you're still intent on ..."

"Of *course* I'm still intent on breaking the curse."

"I will see you at dawn, then."

The Beast left, and I turned my attention to Betty. She looked dreadfully pale. Particularly for one whose complexion is usually so ruddy. A jug of water floated into the room and settled on the bedside table. "Is that you, Molly?" The pen on my bureau rose into the air and began writing on the pad next to it. The pad floated over and hovered under my nose. It read, 'Yes, it's me. The master's been in *such* a rage since last night. We feared that after he destroyed the ship, he might tear the palace down brick by brick.'

"The blame for this lies with me. My late return. But all is well again now. At least, I hope it is …" I said, taking Betty's hand in my own.

'Who is she?' was scratched out on the pad.

"This is Betty. She's been my closest friend for as long as I can remember and …" I was silenced mid-sentence by the sight of the freckles on Betty's face or, should I say, the *lack* of freckles. "Betty, wake up …" I said, clutching her shoulder and shaking it gently. Betty opened her eyes, and she smiled at me. Then, remembering the Beast, she sat upright and gazed about the room.

"It's okay. The Beast isn't here," I said with a reassuring smile.

"I … I knew he was a *beast* …" she said breathlessly, "but …"

"It's true that he can appear quite menacing when you first see him but …"

"*Quite* menacing?"

"Okay. *Rather* menacing. But you'll quickly grow accustomed to him."

"I'll take your word for …" She gasped at something over my shoulder. "What's that!?"

I glanced behind me. "Oh, that's just the pen and pad that Molly's uses to communicate. Remember? The curse I told you about? All the servants are invisible and silent."

Betty nodded and lay her head back on the pillow.

"What are you *doing* here, Betty?" I asked, sounding like a headmistress.

"I couldn't let you return alone. I just couldn't, so …"

"You stole away in the luggage compartment?"

"I thought it for the best," said Betty defiantly. "Aren't you happy to see me?"

"Yes, of course. What's more, the Beast said you are welcome to stay as long as you like."

"It, I mean, *he* did? Even after I fainted at the sight of him?"

"He is nothing if not understanding, it seems."

"I'm starting to feel more than a little guilty," said Betty sheepishly.

"That doesn't surprise me at all. You wouldn't be you otherwise. Betty?"

"Yes?"

"Is a little guilty *all* you're feeling only …?"

"Only what? Why are you looking at me like that? Is there something on my face?" she said, rubbing at her cheek.

"No. Quite the opposite actually. It's your freckles; they …"

"They what?" A mirror floated over from the dressing table and hovered before Betty's inquisitive face. "… My freckles … where are they? And … why am I so *pale*?" We heard the pen scratching out words upon the pad and glanced anxiously at one another. The pad floated about to face us. It read: 'Excuse the impertinence but isn't Betty your servant?'

I nodded. "But first and foremost, she is my *friend*."

'It will not matter. If she's a servant then, now she is here, the curse will make her like the rest of us.'

Betty held her hands before her face. "… It's true, Beauty! I'm *vanishing* …" Indeed, her hands shimmered like a mirage in a desert, and her voice sounded smaller somehow, more distant. I grasped her vanishing shoulders. "In the morning, the Beast and I are departing to find the witch that placed this curse, and I will do *whatever* it takes to remove it. This my solemn promise to you, to *all* of you," I said over my shoulder.

"I have faith in you …" said Betty, her voice so tiny, and then she vanished before my eyes.

Journal entry no. 18

Last night was the worst I can remember. When dawn arrived, I had not slept a wink. I rolled onto the spot where Betty had vanished the night before, shuddered and gazed at the phantoms that my imagination had projected into every corner of my room. I climbed out of bed and, stealing myself, dressed for the adventure that lay ahead.

The rose petals that had, on the previous day, led me to the dock were still scattered in abundance, and once or twice, I was grateful for the reminder of the route.

When I reached the dock, I came upon the Beast carrying a large crate aboard the lifeboat. The boat, while capable of holding a couple of dozen people, was dwarfed by the ship that the Beast had made unseaworthy the day before. Seeing my approach, he placed the crate down at the boat's stern and stepped back onto the dock. "Pray, did you sleep well?" he asked, extending a hand to help me climb aboard.

"Thank you. Not a wink," I said, stepping down into the boat which rocked a little. When the Beast followed me on board, the boat rocked considerably more, and I was grateful for the few seconds he'd allowed me to seat myself. He sat down on the bench opposite my own (ours, the innermost benches of a dozen) and took up the oars. The Beast looked decidedly embarrassed at how awkward his bulk made him and, sensing my thoughts, said, "I don't suppose I shall ever get used to being so clumsy."

"How perceptive you are," I observed with a smile.

He pulled the oars through the water, and the boat glided from the dock. "Do *you* ever get used to it?" he asked.

"Oh, yes," I nodded, "I embraced my own clumsiness long ago."

"That is not what I meant," replied the Beast, looking out over the lagoon.

"Then what did you mean?"

"I was speaking of your … beauty."

I felt myself blushing. "My name has not been an easy one to live up to."

"Hardly surprising," sighed the Beast, pulling on his oars.

I braced myself for some long overdue home truths. "Why hardly surprising?" I asked.

"Your beauty is far from skin deep, and has prevented you from being vain enough to recognise it."

"Oh, I see," I said, looking away from his gaze and reddening.

Sensing my embarrassment, the Beast once again proved his powers of perception by drawing the spotlight back upon himself. "I can see *only too well* how well my own name suits me," he said.

I shook my head. "If only you could see yourself as I see you, you would know that your name was poorly chosen ..." The gentle rocking and swaying of the boat caused me to yawn.

"You will find a blanket at the bow, beside the crate. May I suggest that you take it and make yourself comfortable," said the Beast, motioning to the front of the boat behind me. "Catching up on some much-needed sleep will stand you in good stead."

"All right, I will ..." I said, standing. "And if you don't mind my asking, what's inside the crate?"

"At present? Nothing."

"So, what's it for?"

"I should have thought that obvious."

"Actually, no."

The Beast pulled more forcibly on his oars. "Do you imagine that any ship will make itself available for hire if they see that *I* am a passenger?"

"Oh, *please* don't tell me that the crate is for you?"

The Beast nodded. "Who else?"

"But you are not *cargo*."

"I am not *people* either."

"Nonsense! Of course you're a person."

"It is kind of you to say so; however, I fear that the crew of any ship will not see me as such."

I looked at the crate. "Just how long do you intend to spend inside it?"

"Our journey to the caves, where I believe we will discover the witch's lair, will take two days at most."

"You mean to spend two *days* inside a box?"

"What is two days when compared to the many decades that my brother has spent banished?"

"Your commitment to your brother becomes you. Your mind is made up?"

"It is."

I made my way to the bow of the boat, lay down on some cushions there and pulled the blanket over me. The gentle rocking of the boat, coupled with the rhythmic splash of the oars, sent me into a deep sleep.

In the most vivid of dreams, I found myself returned to the Beast's palace. I was standing in a fabulous ballroom where guests were attending a ball. The smiles and laughter of these people as they danced to the music of an orchestra was infectious, and as I swayed to a waltz, I wished with all my heart that I had a partner to dance with. My wish was granted when the dancers moved aside, opening a path to the other side of the ballroom where a young man stood with his back to me. He was wearing a white uniform and looked so gallant standing in the veranda's open doors. I willed him to turn and face me and, as though able to read my thoughts, he did so. When I saw that it was the Prince, I was overcome with a longing that sent me skirting across the room, and as though possessed of a single mind, he ran towards me. We came together in the centre of the ballroom where he picked me up and twirled me around. He lowered me back down, offered me his arm and then led me the length and breadth of that ballroom in the most enchanting of waltzes. While the room whirled around me, the Prince's face remained in perfect focus. They say that beauty is in the eye of the beholder, and to my eyes, he was the most beautiful of all men. What is more, I felt, *knew* somehow, that his Beauty was not only skin deep but a reflection of his soul.

"You are really here …" he breathed.

"And would not wish to be anywhere else on Earth!"

"In that, we agree," he smiled.

"It is very kind of you to say so. Where are we?"

"In my ballroom during happier times. Before the arrival of the witch."

I stopped dancing and, having taken a step back, searched the other guests as they danced about us. "… Where is he?" I murmured.

"What's wrong? Who else do you seek?" asked the Prince.

"I should have thought that obvious … your brother …"

"My *brother*?"

"Yes. The Beast. Why is he not here?"

The Prince looked none the wiser.

"You *cannot* be ashamed of him! Surely, you can't. He's your own flesh and blood."

"No but ..."

I nodded. "He's ashamed of himself?" I turned, and as I did so, the guests stopped dancing to reveal a clear path to the door. As I walked down it, the Prince called out, "Where are you going, Beauty? You have only just arrived."

"I must find him!" I replied over my shoulder. "*No one* should be alone on a night such as this."

I found myself back in the main entrance hall. A glance in the direction of the Prince's portrait revealed that it had been replaced by another. I approached it slowly, disbelievingly at first, but my heart filled with such joy to see that it was a portrait of the Beast. He was sat beside a table, upon which lay a beautiful rose. "Your portrait has been given pride of place. So why do you hide?" I murmured. "Where are you? Oh, I know! The library. Of course, that is where I will find you."

I made my way to the library, the sound of music and laughter growing ever more distant, and arrived upon the balcony. I could see that someone was seated in the Beast's chair before the fireplace. I imagined it must be him, slumped, reading an improving tone. I moved swiftly down the winding stairs that led to the ground floor, intent on convincing him to return to the ball with me. I placed a hand on the back of the chair and skirted around it only to discover that it was not the Beast ... but the Prince! I woke with a start and sat up. The Beast was pulling on the oars that sent our boat gliding across the water. I climbed unsteadily to my feet and returned to my seat.

"You slept well?" he asked.

I nodded. "But I had the most curious of dreams …"

"Of my brother again?" he asked, pausing his stroke.

"Yes. And of you …"

"Me?"

"Yes. In the dream, I had been transported back in time to happier days at the palace."

The Beast sighed, pulled on his oars and said, "How I would have liked to have joined you."

"There was a ball taking place … the music and dancing were divine."

"And my brother was enjoying himself?"

I nodded. "We danced together until I realised that someone important was missing."

The Beast looked none the wiser. "Surely, there is no one more important to you than my brother."

I looked at him, trying to comprehend if he was truly unaware that the important person of which I spoke was him. And do you know, I think he really was. "How you must have suffered to feel so insignificant," I said.

"Why do you say so?"

"Don't you see? The person of whom I speak, the *important person,* is you."

"… You sought *me* at the palace?"

"I did."

"But you did not find me," he said with a strange certainty.

"Well, yes and no. The portrait of your brother, the one that takes pride of place in the hall, had been replaced with a portrait of you."

"Which only goes to prove that dreams are incredible things where impossible things happen."

"After that, I looked for you in the library. And imagine my surprise when I discovered your brother, who I had left in the ballroom only *minutes* before, seated in your chair." My words seemed to cast the Beast's gaze as adrift as out boat upon that vast lake.

Journal entry no. 19

An hour later, the lights of a port could be seen twinkling in the distance.

"What's it called?" I asked, squinting in its direction.

"The Port of Darkest Skulduggery."

"Are you joking?"

The Beast thought about that for a moment. "It will come as no surprise to you that I have not made a joke in some time."

"Actually, it doesn't. But I have never heard of such a port."

The Beast nodded. "So much of the land is kept secret from us, until it becomes our destiny to find it."

"That's very profound. But, I'm not entirely sure how I feel about the *Port of Darkest Skulduggery* being part of my destiny."

"You are right to be … concerned."

The blanket was draped around my shoulders, and I pulled it tighter about me.

"Although," the Beast began, "I have no doubt that you are more than up to any challenges it holds."

"Thank you. I hope you're right. So, what's the plan?"

"Once I have found a secluded place to moor, I will enter the crate, and you will seal me inside."

"Your mind is made up?" I said, looking over my shoulder at it.

"My appearance makes it necessary."

"All right. And then what?"

"I will give you a purse of gold to hire us a ship and crew willing to take us to our destination."

I braced myself. "And what is the name of our destination?"

"The Caverns of No Return."

"I see. And there's obviously no point in asking if you're joking."

"None."

"Well, at least the name of the caves is self-explanatory. Although, given their name, it doesn't bode particularly well for my convincing someone to take me there."

"Under normal circumstances, I would agree but ..."

"But?"

"The port where we are headed is not known as the Port of Darkest Skulduggery for nothing. The criminals, rogues and pirates to be found there will accept *any* commission so long as the price is right. And I will provide you with all the gold coin you require."

"That's just … *great*," I said with a shudder.

The nearer we drew to the port, the more fitting its name seemed. Indeed, the aggressive shouts, drunken singing of bawdy songs, and shattering of glass sent a chill down my spine.

Not long after, we entered a canal where the backs of shops and inns rose around us. The sounds I have already mentioned were joined by gunfire, threats of violence, and the barking of ferocious dogs.

"I will allow no harm to come to you," said the Beast with such conviction that I believed him.

"Or I you," I replied.

"I do not doubt it."

The Beast moored our boat in a quiet spot, a good distance from any gas lamps, and climbed past me to the crate. The crate, which stood as high as his waist, had a hinged front which he opened to reveal the space within.

"Will you even *fit* in there?" I asked, joining him at the front of the boat.

"Yes. And with a little room to spare."

"You could have fooled me," I murmured as I gazed inside it.

The Beast took a red purse from his belt and handed it to me.

"How much is *in* here …" I asked as the weight of the purse pulled my arm down to my side.

"Fifty gold coins. I have chosen this inn for a reason," he said, motioning to the crooked wooden building that towered over us. "It's a well-known haunt for those with boats for hire."

"Splendid," I replied, securing the purse to my belt which sagged on that side. The Beast climbed inside the crate and, having lowered himself down, looked for all the world like the biggest fluffy toy ever made. "Are you *sure* you're going to be okay in there?" I asked.

"Fear not. For one of the perks of being a beast is hardiness. Now seal me inside and hire us a boat."

"I will not let you down …"

"I know."

I closed the lid which sealed with a meaty clunk and gazed up at the inn.

Journal entry no. 20

The Port of Darkest Skulduggery? As I opened the door to the Inn, it occurred to me that I was standing in the doorway to the *Inn* of Darkest Skulduggery. I could at least take comfort from the fact that I had visited such places in books many times.

I am not a fish that's completely *out of water*, I thought, walking inside.

Having stepped nimbly around some patrons dancing an uproarious jig to an out of tune piano, I observed a dozen tables where pirates either arm wrestled or gambled at cards. All were as drunk as skunks and looked a good deal smellier. As for the ladyfolk, well, let's just say that their behaviour is best left to the imagination. A drunken oaf raised a tankard to his lips and so eager was he to transfer its contents to his stomach that he threw back his head, lost his balance and trod on my foot. I howled in agony, but such was the din in that establishment that not a soul heard me. I limped towards the bar where several men were studying papers laid out there. Having chosen the man who looked the soberest, I forced my way through the fray and squeezed in against the bar beside him. He was gazing down at a map.

"Excuse me," I said.

The man, whose bushy black beard must have been exceedingly itchy, for he scratched ferociously at it, was either deaf or chose not to hear me. "Sir!" I said, undeterred, "I need to hire a boat and crew. Can you help me?"

The man looked up, not at me but the barman and, in the hoarsest voice that I had ever heard called out, "Another bottle of yer finest rum!" The barman nodded, and the man looked back down at his map. I have no idea what possessed me, but I placed an arm upon it, obscuring an X that so fascinated him. This unexpected obstruction of the X certainly got his attention. Unfortunately, I cannot report his initial words to me, as they would be out of place in this journal. Once he'd finished bellowing in my face, I wiped his spittle from my chin.

"I have come here to hire a boat and crew!" I bellowed back at him. "And what's more," I continued, "I have gold coin enough to pay MOST HANDSOMELY." The look on his weather-beaten face led me to believe that had he not heard the words 'gold' and 'coin' in that order, I would not have been able to make any further entries in this journal due to my arms being ripped from their sockets.

"*Gold coin*?" he growled.

I nodded.

"How much *gold coin*?"

"Fifty pieces to anyone who will deliver me and my cargo to the Caverns of No Return."

The man observed me as though I'd lost every marble I had ever owned and then some. He picked up the bottle the bartender had just placed before him, pulled the cork, drank greedily from it, slammed it down, burped and said, "Did I 'ere you correctly? You seek passage to the Caverns of No Return?"

"Your ears serve you very well," I nodded.

"Well then, it's plain as day that you're a couple of planks short of a full deck, Missy."

"I protest against your observation in the *strongest possible terms.*"

"You can protest all yer like, but that don't make it any less true."

I lifted my arm from his map. "If you're not up to the task, then perhaps you will point me in the direction of someone who is?"

"I didn't say I weren't up to it now ..." he said, grabbing at his beard and extracting a flea which he flicked over my head. In truth, the flea would have been transferred *to* my head had I not ducked.

"Charming. Do you even have a boat?" I asked, straightening up.

"Do I even have a boat, she asks me?" I was about to move away when he took hold of my arm. "I have the biggest, sturdiest boat in these here parts. The real question is, *do you* have any gold coin?"

I lifted the purse that dangled from my belt and held it up where he could see it.

"You mean to tell me that's filled with gold?" he said, casting a furtive glance around the bar.

"It is." A moment later, I was being dragged through the bar towards the door.

Once outside, I protested that he "Unhand me this instant or so help me!"

"All right, quiet down," he said, releasing my arm. "You got any idea what would happen if those villains got whiff of so much gold in their midst?"

"Nothing ventured, nothing gained," I said, raising my chin.

"And did I hear you correct? It's your intention to travel to the Caverns of No Return?" he asked, peering at me.

"It is."

"Those caves were named so for good reason. It's well documented that a powerful witch lives in 'em. Not only powerful but as vindictive as they come. Responsible for many a curse. Yer smiling, which only goes to prove that my earlier observation about yer being several planks short of a full deck was correct."

I shook my head. "I am smiling because she sounds like the very witch I seek. Will you take me to her?"

"No. But for fifty gold coin, I'll take you as close as anyone with their wits about them might."

"And how close might that be?"

"There's a cove that's, oh, little more than a mile from the caverns. So, we have a deal?" he said, spitting on his palm and offering me his hand.

"Yes," I said, spitting on my own and shaking it.

"Well then, I'm going to need an advance of six gold coin."

"Why six?" I asked, wiping my hand on my dress.

"To hire a crew of six that's willin' to embark upon such a journey." Trusting my instincts that I had stumbled upon a trustworthy rogue, I opened my purse, dug out the six coins and handed them over. "And your name is?" I enquired.

"I'm known in these parts as the Captain. Now you stay 'ere while I go back inside and get us a crew."

He emerged some minutes later with six of the meanest looking pirates I had ever seen and responded to my expression by saying, "While they are undoubtedly a bunch of murderous scoundrels, they are also experienced sailors."

"Well then, consider me reassured," I said with no little irony.

One of the scoundrels lifted a bottle of beer to his lips. "A toast to this little lady! It's not often that the likes of us are offered gainful employment by the likes of 'er." There came a chorus of "Here here!" followed by much hearty gulping, swigging and chugging of beer. "My vessel is this way," said the Captain, lurching off.

"Just a minute!" I called after him. "I have cargo, remember? A single crate. It's in a boat that's *this* way," I said, stepping in the opposite direction.

When we arrived at the lifeboat, the Captain instructed his crew to lift out the crate. The burliest two climbed aboard and, having taken hold of the crate, grimaced horribly as they tried and failed to lift it. Standing on the dock, I checked my nails as though butter wouldn't melt in my mouth. The first two pirates were joined by two more, and much huffing and puffing ensued. "She must 'av the crown jewels in 'ere or somfin'! Get down 'ere and give us an 'and, will ya?" said one of them to the remaining two. Thankfully, the six of them could lift it.

The Captain had not lied about his ship. It was the largest in the dock, with a mast that towered high above the others. Once the men had deposited the crate on the deck, they set to work, raising the sail.

When we sailed from port, I was standing beside the Captain at the ship's wheel. "How long will it take us to reach the cove?" I said, glancing over my shoulder at the crate.

"No more than a couple of days, the winds be willing." The Captain, mindful of my interest in the crate, said, "It doesn't actually have the crown jewels in it, does it?"

"Ah, no."

"Whatever is in it, you should know that the men will not carry it to those caves nor anywhere near 'em."

"They need only carry it to a place where I might open it in private."

"Right, you are," he replied, sounding more than a little intrigued by the crate's contents.

"Thank you for helping me and being so understanding."

"You can save yer thanks till I've delivered you and yer cargo safe and sound to yer destination," he said, drawing a shaky hand across his brow.

Diary entry no. 21

I am happy to report that the first 24hrs of our journey passed without incident. The winds were favourable and carried us across that vast gulf of water towards the distant mountains at a good speed. My cabin below deck was spacious, and my bed comfortable enough to make me feel *more* than little guilty about the Beast inside the crate. The next morning, I went up on deck to discover the Captain occupied by a chart, and the crew busy tending the rigging. I moseyed over to the crate and, looking nonchalantly out to sea, tapped my fingers on it. I listened for a tapped reply. None came. But, comforted by the thought that the Beast could break free of his confinement at any time, I felt reassured enough to return to my cabin.

It was when I returned to the deck at dusk that I felt a terrible sense of foreboding. I had intended to stand beside the crate and watch the sun set but noticed that the ship's wheel had been abandoned. It swung back and forth with the passing of the current upon the rudder. I moved swiftly to steady it, but such was the violence of its swings; I thought the better of doing so. The winds picked up, causing the sail to billow and flap above me. I gazed up, eager to see the two of three crew members who usually tended it. "Where *is* everyone …" I murmured. As though in answer to my question, the door that led below to the Captain's cabin burst open and the

Captain came stumbling out. He crashed down upon the deck before me, his face horribly beaten. "I'm sorry …" he mouthed up at me. I was suddenly aware that the crew had gathered around me.

"What is the meaning of this?" I cried.

"Well, it's like this *pretty*," said one, grabbing my chin and forcing me to look into his leering eyes. "We had ourselves a vote and …" I felt myself being spun about whereupon another of the rogues grasped my hair and, having brought his scarred face close to my own, said, "And the upshot of our vote is this: it's too risky goin' so close to 'em caves …" Again, I was manhandled around by another of the crew who added, "But the Captain 'ere would 'ere nothing of our concerns …. and left us little option but to mutiny …" I was spun about again to face the original rogue who added with relish, "which means we'll have to throw him overboard for the sharks to feed on!"

"But you can't!" I protested.

"This is a mutiny, and we'll do as we please, Missy. You see anybody around who can stop us?" Such was the bloodlust in their eyes that I crouched over the Captain to shield him. I must have looked rather comical, for they laughed at me.

"And then there's the matter of them crown jewels …" said the rogue with the scar on his face.

"What crown jewels?" I asked.

They all gazed in the direction of the crate at the ship's stern.

"No! There's *nothing* of value in there if that's why you're doing this."

"We'll be the judge of that," said one as he raised a crowbar and led the others to the crate. The men had no need of their crowbar, as the next moment, I heard the splintering of wood, followed by a terrifying roar, as the Beast made himself known. The Captain, having glanced in their direction, pulled my face down onto his chest. "Don't look …" he breathed as he watched the spectacle with ever-widening eyes. The yells, shrieks and cries that followed were punctuated by several loud splashes, *six* to be precise, whereupon the Captain released his grip on me. I jumped to my feet, and seeing the Beast's heavy breathing silhouette against the moonlit sea, I ran to him. The Beast opened his arms and, drawing me up in them, said, "Have no fear. The danger has passed." As soon as he put me down, I ran to the boat's stern. "… You have thrown them all overboard?"

"I have," replied the Beast, joining me. "Which is no more than they deserved." The boat was moving slowly through the choppy water, and I caught sight of the men splashing about in the distance. I looked up at the Beast. "We can't just let them drown."

"As I said, it's no more than they deserve." I noticed that the Beast's tunic was torn, and his shoulder was bleeding. "You're *hurt* …" I said, taking a handkerchief from my pocket and holding it against his wound.

"It's nothing …" said the Beast quietly, "I suppose you're right about the crew," he sighed.

"So, we go back and pick them up?"

"Absolutely not. There are limits …" He leaned over the back of the boat and untied a lifeboat that hung there. It crashed down into the sea, and the crew, clearly strong swimmers, splashed their way towards it.

"It's more kindness than I would have shown them rascals, and I'm a …" came the voice of the Captain from behind us. Over his shoulder, the Beast said, "And you are what? A *man*?"

We turned to face the Captain whose troubled gaze found me. "I'm hoping and praying that this *creature* is a friend of yours?" he said.

"Rest assured; he is the very *best* of friends. Captain, may I present the Beast; Beast, this is the Captain."

"The Captain has been badly beaten," observed the Beast, "I suggest you tend to his wounds."

"It's nought but a couple of scratches," replied the Captain. "So, Mr Beast …"

"It's just Beast."

"Well then, *Beast*, it will not have escaped your attention that we recently lost our crew."

The Beast looked up at the sail, billowing and flapping in the wind. "It had not."

"You've proven that you have the strength of six men, but do you also have their know-how?"

The Beast gestured to the ship's wheel with his chin. "You take the helm, Captain, and leave the rest to me."

The Captain winked at me. "That is music to my ears," he said, heading for the wheel.

Journal entry no. 22

I went to bed early, and to my immense delight, I heard laughter from the deck above. It had been a long time since the Beast had made a new friend, and at the sound of it, my own spirits must have risen as much as his. I fell asleep with a smile on my face, a smile that vanished as I entered a dream state. I was standing on a high ridge, overlooking a forest, within which a circular tower soared high above the trees. I raised a hand to my eyes to shield from the sun and squinted up at the barred window at its top. The sense of loneliness I felt is hard to convey, as I knew, in my heart of hearts, that it was the place where the Prince had been banished these long years.

I found myself stepping and sliding down a steep embankment, and having reached the forest's floor, as is so often the case with dreams, I was outside the fortress-like tower in an instant. A wooden door at the tower's base opened as though in welcome. I flew through it, desperate to find and reassure the Prince that help was at hand. The winding steps within were seemingly *endless*, and my heart raced as I climbed them, not only with the effort of that steep climb but at the thought of gazing upon his face.

At the top, I discovered another door and, in my eagerness to confirm that it was open, I hurled myself against it. The door did not give way, and I bounced off, clutching my arm. Along with my spirits, I sank to the ground and rested my back against the door. I heard a voice from inside the room behind me. It sounded distant at first, but as it drew nearer, I recognised it as the Prince's.

"Is there someone there?" he asked so disbelievingly that my heart sank.

"It's me! Beauty!" I said, scrambling to my feet.

"Beauty? But how did you find me? This tower is beyond the senses of all. Invisible! And you should *not* be here. It's too dangerous."

I pressed my palms to the door. "I would not wish to be *anywhere* else …"

"At least now you can now see for yourself," said the Prince, thumping hard upon the door, "It *cannot* be opened."

"Your brother *will* open it," I said through gritted teeth.

"My brother?" replied the Prince, once again sounding for all the world as though he had forgotten he had a brother.

"Yes. Your brother *the Beast*. He's on his way!"

"… Yes, yes, of course, but …"

"But nothing. He has the strength of six men, and he will tear down this door …" I said, balling my fists against it.

"Please, do not get your hopes up, Beauty. This door is held closed by powerful magic. So powerful that I suspect it will require more than brute strength of my brother to tear it down."

126

I nodded. "Well then, take heart, for we are on route to speak with the witch."

Silence.

"Are you there?" I asked.

"Know this," began the Prince gravely, "the heart of that hag is as black as oil. You *cannot* expect any mercy from her. And you'll be placing yourself in terrible danger."

"It matters not. I have long since been resolved to do whatever I must to break this curse. If that should result in my own demise, then so be it."

"Beauty ..." sighed the Prince, softly.

"Yes?"

"Then ... then you *must* remember what I told you and look for me not with your eyes but with your ..."

Once again, I awoke with a dreadful start. I felt a pain in my arm where I'd collided with the door and, glancing down, saw that it was bruised. I lay my head down on my pillow and quietened my breathing. "Have no fear, I *will* seek you with my heart. And I will find you."

The following morning, I emerged from below deck to see that dark, fast-moving clouds filled the sky. The Beast was standing at the ship's wheel.

"Good morning. Where is the Captain?" I asked, hugging myself for warmth. The Beast glanced at me over his shoulder. "He has retired to his cabin for some much-needed sleep." A blanket was wrapped around the Beast's shoulders. He removed it with a flourish and draped it tenderly across my own. While the blanket had barely covered his chest, it positively swamped me. "Are you certain you don't need your blanket?" I smiled up at him.

"Yes, quite certain," he replied in a voice made purposely deep. "As you can see, I am large and ugly enough to cope with a chill wind."

"Apparently not," I murmured, pulling the blanket tight around me.

The Beast cleared his throat. "You have injured your arm?"

"Apparently so. Curiously, it happened in a dream."

"Maybe it is not so curious," said the Beast philosophically.

"What do you mean?"

"I have read a paper by an eminent scientist which states that those things we encounter in our dreams can also manifest themselves … why are you looking at me like *that*?" he asked.

"Like what?"

"Like I have said something … endearing."

I shrugged. "I spoke with your brother in my dream and injured my arm against the door which separated us."

"I see. And what did my *brother* have to say for himself?"

"What *is it* with you two? Whenever you speak of each other, you do so in the vaguest of terms."

"I … I don't know what you mean."

"It's as though you keep *forgetting* one another."

"It has been a great many years since …"

"Yes, I know, since the witch separated you."

"So?" sighed the Beast. "What did my brother have to say for himself?"

"He was concerned for my safety. *Particularly* when I told him we were on our way to find the witch."

"It pleases me to hear that he was concerned. Tell me, where was this door that separated you both?"

"That's a really good question …" I smiled.

"I have my moments."

"I've noticed," I said and felt myself reddening. "I came upon the door at the top of a tower."

"A tower?"

"Yes. A tower in the middle of a vast forest."

"Isolated?"

"I'll say. It was perhaps the loneliest place on Earth. Please, do not look so downcast. We are going to free him from that dreadful place."

"I wish I had your faith."

"Right now, I wish I had your fur," I shuddered.

Journal entry no. 23

The Captain joined us on deck at midday and took control of the ship's wheel. The storm had worsened, its winds now powerful enough to blow *anything* that had not been tied down overboard. We spent the hours that followed in quiet contemplation of what lay ahead.

At dusk, the Captain informed us that we would soon be arriving at our destination. The Beast and I had been standing at the ship's bow, watching for glimpses of shore illuminated by lightning. The Beast turned to face the Captain at his wheel. "Where is this cove at which you're going to drop us?" he asked.

"There's been a change plan," replied the Captain.

"Oh, yes?" said the Beast.

The Captain smiled. "I'm taking you directly to your destination. As close as I can get."

I turned to face the Captain. "There really is no need. That was not what we agreed."

"A lot has changed since then."

"True. But you cannot hold yourself responsible for what the crew did," I said.

"In that, we are in agreement," said the Beast.

The Captain tightened his grasp on his wheel, "That's just somethin' we'll have to agree to disagree on, then."

"That's very kind of you, Jim," said the Beast.

"*Jim?*" I said, looking back and forth between them.

"Jim's my name. And only those I consider my friends get to know or call me it."

"Does that include me?" I asked.

"It does."

"Thank you, Jim. I am Beauty."

"True. And if you'd rather not tell me your name, I understand."

"No. Beauty *is* my name," I said, rolling my eyes.

The Captain furrowed his brow. "Beauty and the *Beast?*"

The Beast and I glanced awkwardly at one another. "That about sums us up," murmured the Beast.

Jim steered the ship into a cove where cliffs gathered about us. He dropped the anchor and then went to the aft of the boat where he called to the Beast to help him lower a raft. Not long after, we looked down upon the raft, bobbing up and down on the water. Jim unhooked a lantern from a pole and, having handed it to the Beast, offered me a hand. I imagined he intended to help me climb down into the raft. I was, therefore, taken aback when he shook my hand warmly. "You're a remarkable young woman, and I wish you all the luck in the world," he said.

"Thank you, Jim."

"And you be sure to take good care of the Beast," he said, looking up at him.

"I will allow no harm to come to him," I replied.

"I don't doubt it. I will be here when you return."

"Give us twenty-four hours," said the Beast, "if we have not returned, then it is unlikely we ever shall."

"That's a bit glum," I said.

The Beast stroked his chin. "Not necessarily. We may be forced to take another mode of transport home."

Jim shook his head. "This is an *island*."

"Yes. But this is no ordinary island. It's a place where anything is possible. Be that thing good or …"

"Why not leave it at that?" I said.

The Beast nodded and extended a paw to Jim. Man and Beast shook hands, and the Beast climbed down into the lifeboat. He looked up, opened his arms, and I climbed down into them.

Jim watched, arms folded, as the Beast rowed us towards the cove's sandy shore. By the time we reached it, all that was visible of the ship were two distant lamps that burned like tiny fireflies. Our own little boat slid up upon the sand, and once we had climbed out, the Beast held aloft the lantern. It illuminated a great many boulders that had been arranged to form a staircase to a plateau above. I stepped towards these 'stairs' and felt the Beast take hold of my arm. "Even now, it is not too late to change your mind," he said.

I looked up at the Beast's face illuminated by the flickering lamplight. "Change it? More than ever, I am *determined* to face the witch."

"Why more than ever?" he asked.

"Because ... because I *know you* now."

"When you say me, you mean my brother?"

"*No*. While it is true that I would *very much* like to get to know your brother better, I barely know him at all."

"And the reason you are so determined to get to him better?"

I sighed. "I am loathed to say it aloud for fear that you will think me shallow."

"You *care* what I think of you? When I am nothing but ..."

I stood on tiptoes, reached up, and placed a hand across his mouth. "*Please*, do not speak ill of yourself."

The Beast nodded, and I removed my hand. "Let's go and find this witch," I said with as much determination as I could muster.

Once we'd reached the top of the staircase, a staircase that the Beast explained had been made by smugglers in centuries past, we emerged onto a small plateau. Before us, we saw an opening between two rock faces, one wide enough for a single horse and rider to pass through. In the light of the Beast's raised lamp, we could see that the passage beyond went on for some distance. Unfortunately, that is not all we saw in that creeping lamplight, as stuck on pikes were human skulls, their faces arranged so that they scowled in our direction. I swallowed so hard it was practically a gulp. "Who *were* these poor souls?" I breathed.

"I have done my research and *know* who they were ..."

"Well?"

"I would prefer not to say, as knowing will only cause you undue distress. But," the Beast sighed, "since you are here, and it's your intention to proceed further, then you have a right to know." The Beast's words had set the cat chasing pigeons in my mind. "These heads," I began bravely, "did they once sit upon the shoulders of *other* good Samaritans? Those who have attempted to talk to the witch on your behalf?"

My words must have had the most extraordinary effect, for the Beast threw back his head, and for the first time, I heard his throaty laughter. Not being accustomed to laughter, he then had a coughing fit. I thudded him on the back and, once he had stopped, cradled my aching arm.

"I do ... I do believe that you could raise the spirits of the dead," he said, wiping the tears from his eyes.

"I take it; these are not the heads of previous good Samaritans, then?"

"It is doubtful there are *this* many good Samaritans in all the Land. And if I had lured them all here, knowing the fate that awaited them, I would be a beast by name *and* nature." The very notion of having done such a thing gave him cause to shudder.

"So, who are these unfortunate souls, then?" I asked.

"They are the kidnapped victims of the pirates who inhabited these caves long before the witch. She doubtless leaves them to deter visitors."

I nodded my approval of his explanation. "Shall we?" I said, indicating the path ahead. The Beast squeezed through the opening, and I followed closely in his footsteps.

Not long after we reached the cavern's entrance, and as we stepped over its threshold, a rancid stench climbed my nostrils.

"Bats," said the Beast, raising a hand to his nose.

"Really? I had no idea bats smelled so dreadful …"

"You misunderstand me. Bat *dung*. This way …" he said, stepping in the direction of a passage through the rock on our right-hand side. There was a passage on the left-hand side also. "How can you be certain that *that* way leads to the witch?" I asked.

"My research has been thorough."

"But who would know such things?"

The Beast sighed. "A sailor was captured and enslaved by the witch."

"He escaped?"

"No. But he was able to send word of his plight."

"How?"

"The witch keeps homing pigeons. They allow her to communicate with her siblings."

"The witch has siblings?"

"Two sisters. Both are witches."

"Well then, that's something the witch and I have in common."

"Are you suggesting that your sisters are witches?"

"No. To do so would be out of character. I wasn't called Beauty for nothing," I mused, "although, having said that, I think it *very* fortunate that my sisters don't possess supernatural powers."

"Tell me about them ..." said the Beast as he stepped towards the passage and beckoned me to follow.

"I know what you're doing," I said.

"Doing?"

"You're trying to distract me, take my mind off the witch's den we have come to find."

"Am I really so transparent to you?"

"You really are ..." We were halted in our tracks by the sound of laughter. The laughter was comfortingly distant yet, at the same time, and without wishing to pass judgement on another's way of expressing mirth, more of a deranged cackle.

"Shall we," said the Beast, putting his best foot forward and indicating that I do the same. "We really should be buoyed by this happy evidence," he continued, referring to the cackle.

"Oh, yes?" I replied.

"Of course. It's an indication that we have come to the right place."

I nodded. "And do you recognise the laughter?"

"Not as such. You see, the witch did not have much cause for laughter that night."

"What? Not even after she placed her curse?"

"Not even then."

"You surprise me."

"Why do you say so?"

"I have read many stories that feature evil witches, and in all but the most exceptional of cases, it is quite common for witches to cackle with delight after cursing someone."

"Which goes to prove two things: firstly, that this is the most exceptional of cases and, secondly, that you should not believe all you read in stories."

"I couldn't agree more. And that is *precisely* why I have been keeping a journal."

"You jest," replied the Beast, either unwilling or unable to believe his ears. "And now," he went on, "it is my turn to say how transparent you are to me."

"I am?"

"Yes. You are trying to take my mind off our perilous situation just as I was."

"How well you know me," I said as we turned a bend in the tunnel. We were halted in our tracks by the sight of a well-lit cavern some fifty metres away. I wiped my sweaty palms on my dress, cleared my throat and said, "Now *those* are typical of stories I've read about witches."

"Those?" asked the Beast.

"Yes. Gigantic shadows thrown up upon a wall. In this instance, shadows cast by *three* witches."

The Beast raised his torch. "I do believe that your use of the plural is correct."

"I'm certain of it. Perhaps her sisters have come for a visit."

"A perfect time for a family reunion," sighed the Beast.

"It sounds as though they are squabbling amongst themselves," I said as we marshalled our courage and stepped towards their den.

"Quite so. And now the time has come for us to stop trying to calm each other's nerves and …"

"And face up to the challenge of appealing to the goodwill of not just one but *three* evil witches."

"Quite so," swallowed the Beast.

Diary entry no. 24

When we entered their den, the witches were *so* engrossed in a conversation about the ingredients of their caldron they didn't notice they had visitors. This provided us an opportunity to take in their cavernous home. It was spacious enough to contain several cottages and yet, with its many burning torches, also warm and cosy. But its décor left *much* to be desired. The rib cages of several large sea mammals had been converted into sofas. The cushions upon them had been made from dead animals stuffed with leaves that protruded from every orifice. Indeed, if their den had a theme, it would be *dead animals of the forest*. Piled high against the walls were hundreds of pitiable creatures waiting to be used for those activities usually associated with witches: sacrifices, potions, poisons, and the telling of fortunes. On the right-hand side of their den was a blood-stained altar illuminated by hundreds of candles. The candles burned so brightly that they left stars in my eyes. I looked back to where the witches, having settled on the correct ingredient, now ladled it into their caldron from a bucket suspended above it. As we drew nearer, one of the witches raised her nose and sniffed at the air. "What *is* that stench?" she asked her two companions. In response, they sniffed at the air in a similarly deranged manner. "It's *disgusting*!" spat one.

"Quite revolting! The despicable stench of ..."

"A beast," sighed the Beast.

"Of innocence!" barked the centre witch.

"Worse ... of kindness," exclaimed the third, wrinkling her nose in disgust, "and of ... *beauty*," she continued as all three turned slowly, almost disbelievingly, to face us.

"What have we here, sisters?" said the centre witch, her voice raspy and cutting.

The witch to her right rung her hands as though the sight of us boded well for their pot. "Guests!" she hissed.

"And aren't they a sight for sore eyes!" The sisters were identical twins: beak-like noses, large moles on their chins and foreheads, and dark, murderous eyes that never once blinked. The Beast stepped in front of me and, extending an arm to prevent my passing, said, "We mean you no harm and have come only to talk."

"*Talk?*" chirped the centre witch as though unfamiliar with the word.

"Yes. And to one of you in particular," I said, stepping around the Beast and standing by his side.

The witch on the left drew a filthy rag from her belt and placed it over her nose. "And who might you be?" she asked with a grimace.

"My name is Beauty. And this is my friend the Beast."

Her dead eyes widened. "Beauty and the *Beast?*"

"That's us," I said, glancing up at him.

The witches went into a huddle and whispered furiously to one another.

"And … and *your* names are?" I asked, raising my voice.

They stopped whispering, just long enough to glance in my direction, as though to check that I was indeed there, and then recommenced their whispering with greater fury.

I cleared my throat and, marshalling greater courage still, said, "When visitors introduce themselves, it's customary to do the same in return." The witches broke their huddle, and what had looked like an enormous black raven split suddenly into three smaller crows. The witch on the left cocked her head at me "My name is Martha."

"Maude," rasped the centre witch.

"Marris," joined the third.

The Beast took a step towards them. "I have met one of you before now," he said, scrutinising them.

"Indeed, you have …" said Maude.

"But which is the witch you met?" asked Martha.

"And what is your business with her?" hissed Marris. All three stood with their heads cocked to the right like inquisitive statues in a house of horrors.

"It is *impossible* to tell which I met …" said the Beast.

"But your other question is easy to answer," I said, taking a step towards them. "*One* of you came upon the Beast's palace and cursed its inhabitants."

Martha, Maude, and Marris nodded in unison.

"Your curse made the servants invisible and dumb and …"

"*And?*" asked Maude, cocking her head further still.

"And it banished the Beast's brother, imprisoning him somewhere beyond the reach and tenderness of others."

Marris narrowed her eyes at the Beast. "His *Brother?*"

The Beast stepped forwards urgently and said, "I must *insist* that you allow me to speak with you in private."

"You are not in your palace now!" barked Martha.

"And it would, therefore, be foolish to insist on anything!" said Maude.

The Beast clasped his hands together. "Then I *implore you,* speak with me in private, beyond the ears of Beauty."

"But why?" I asked.

"My dear," said Marris, "it seems your friend has been keeping secrets from you."

"Secrets regarding the *true* nature of the curse," said Maude, glancing left and right at her sisters.

"Is this *true?*" I asked the Beast.

He turned to face me and nodded gravely. "I ask that you trust me. For if we have even a *flicker* of a chance of breaking this curse, then ..." The Beast looked at me so imploringly that I could do little else but nod.

"The *flicker* of a chance," cackled Maude.

"Indeed," said Marris. "Looking at the monstrous creature that stands before us now, it is rather *less* than a flicker!"

The Beast turned his troubled gaze upon the witches. "Even though it may be one chance in a billion, *please* ... just let me discuss it with you in private."

The witches glanced at one another, and then extended their arms towards me with such venom that, fearing I was about to breathe my last, I closed my eyes. I opened them a moment later to find myself standing in the cove where our boat was moored. Feeling a mixture of injustice, curiosity and fear, not only for myself but the Beast, I sprinted along the sand, climbed the rocky stairs, and flew along the passage past the skulls.

I arrived back in the den to see the Beast conferring with the witches. Upon my approach, the conspirators nodded in agreement, and the Beast backed away from them. I went to his side and said, "I object in the strongest possible terms to being ... to being *banished* in such a way."

"Well then, imagine how my brother must have felt all these years," sighed the Beast. I am pleased to say that his words had quite the sobering effect upon me. "Yes, yes, *of course*. Please forgive me. So, you have made your bargain then?"

"We have made a bargain of sorts," said the Beast miserably, "but believe me when I tell you it is no more than was promised by one of the sisters on that fateful night."

Maude stepped forwards. "Agreed our bargain? Not *quite*."

"But you just agreed," growled the Beast.

"We shall agree to it but only if Beauty can choose which one us was refused sanctuary."

"Yes!" hissed Marris gleefully, "which one of us placed the curse? Choose correctly, and we will fulfil our agreement and give the Beast its one in a billion chance of breaking the curse."

"But choose *poorly,* and the agreement will be void, and even that one in a billion chance will be no more."

"What is the meaning of this?" asked an increasingly flustered Beast.

"Come now, Beast, you would not deprive we three sisters a little fun, surely?" said Maude.

"I would when so much is at stake."

I stepped forwards, and casting a glance over the three witches, top to *toe*, I said, "I accept the challenge gladly, and I hereby choose ..."

"Beauty!" cried the Beast, "how can you be so reckless?"

"I do not believe I am ... I choose *Marris*," I said, darting a glance at her.

Marris balled her hands into fists and, having placed them irritably on her hips, said, "Are there *four* witches here?"

"So, Beauty has chosen *correctly*," said the Beast.

Maude fixed her gaze on me. "She has, but how? And with such certainty?"

"I'm no witch. I just remembered something the Beast said in passing about your feet," I said, glancing down at them.

The Beast swallowed hard. "In my agitated state, even I had overlooked that detail."

"Well then, it's time!" said Marris.

"Time for what?" I asked.

"For you to embark upon the impossible challenge that the Beast has arranged for you. So, come closer, *Beauty* ..." said Maude, beckoning me with a crooked finger.

I glanced up at the Beast.

"It's okay. Go to her. She has something she must give you."

I took three strides and stood before the witches.

"Take *this*," hissed Maude, extending her arms. Laid across her hands was a silver chain, about a metre in length, with fist-sized hoops at either end.

"What's it for?" I asked, lifting it.

"You are to be transported to the Tower of Solitude," said the Beast quietly from behind me.

"Where?" I asked, examining the silver chain more closely.

The Beast cleared his throat. "It is the place where you last visited the Prince."

"The Tower of Solitude? The name is an apt one ..." I murmured.

"Once there," said Marris, "you must place one of the hoops around the Prince's right wrist, and the other around your left ..."

"Tethering you to the Prince," said the Beast.

"But why?" I said, glancing at him over my shoulder.

Martha lifted a rag to her nose to mask my stench. She leaned in close and said spitefully, "To break my sister's curse, you must remain tethered to the Prince until you have crossed the River of Lost Souls. If you're able to accomplish this feat, then the curse will be lifted."

"Then we shall remain tethered," I said defiantly. "But how will I get through the door into his cell?"

"You will find the door open," said the Beast. I turned and, looking up at him, saw that he was trembling. "There is no need to be *quite* so nervous. I intend to stay tethered to your brother if it's the *last* thing I do." Strangely, the Beast looked at me as though he did not doubt it. I say strangely because it was as though he feared that I would stay true to my word.

I stepped towards him. "I have no idea what concerns you, of the secret pact you have made with the sisters, but you must trust me," I said.

"I will if ..."

"If?"

"If you'll trust your heart. If you do not, I fear this may be the last time I gaze upon your face …"

"I *will* trust it."

"Come what may?" asked the Beast.

"Come what may," I repeated.

"Enough of this loathsome talk!" screeched Maude, and all went dark.

Journal entry no. 25

Seconds later, light filled my vision, a cascade of jumbled colours that formed a whole picture … and there, through the open door to his cell, sat the Prince. He looked up at me as though unable to believe his eyes and then, having resolved to discover if I was real, scrambled to his feet. We came together in the middle of his cell, and whatever he was about to say was replaced by "Why are you tethering us together?"

I looked up into his eyes, so imploring, so beautiful, and once I had managed to draw breath, I said, "Do you trust me?"

The Prince almost shrugged but, seeing the determination on my face, nodded.

"Good," I swallowed. "Then *believe* me when I tell you that to break the curse that has banished you to a lifetime of loneliness, we need only stay tethered until we have crossed the River of Lost Souls."

The Prince gazed through the open door. "Then, I'm free to leave? The witch will not find and return me?"

I shook my head. "It was she who set us this challenge. Come on!" I said, leading him from his cell. When we reached the top of the winding stairs, the tower began to shudder as though from a powerful earthquake.

"We must hurry!" I said.

"What's happening?" asked the Prince as we ran down the winding stairs side by side.

"You're leaving the tower, so … so perhaps the witches have no further use for it?"

"Then what is to become of me if we fail?"

"We won't fail. We cannot!"

We reached the tower's base in the nick of time, for as we flew through the door into the forest, it started to crumble to the ground behind us. The Prince took hold of my hand, the one already tethered to his own, and we ran into the forest until the sound of stone crashing down on stone had faded from earshot.

"I can scarce believe it!" he said, slowing me to a halt. He turned and looked back to where the tower *would* have been visible above the trees.

"Believe it," I panted, "you are free, and will never again have to return to that place."

"And I have you to thank for this," he said, taking my hands in his.

"I … I have played my role, but I would *never* have managed it alone, not without the help of your brother. And the curse is not yet broken …" I said, glancing at the tethers around our wrists.

The Prince held my hands to his cheek. "In the short time that it will take us to reach the River of Lost Souls, what force of nature could *possibly* force us to separate?"

"I cannot imagine one …"

The Prince glanced up at the sun low in the sky to the east where it would soon set. "We must cover as much ground as possible before dusk. And then build a fire big enough to keep them at bay …"

"Keep *what* at bay?" I asked, glancing about.

The Prince lowered my hands. "One of the few comforts I had during my captivity has now become a threat. You see, the forest … it is home to a pack of ravenous wolves," he said, placing his free arm around my waist and pulling me close.

"I see," I breathed, happy for him to do so.

"We must, therefore, build a fire before dark. It is the only thing that will keep them at bay. To that end, we should make haste and get as close to our goal as possible before sunset."

"Agreed."

So it was that hand in tethered hand, we made haste, the sinking sun upon our backs, towards the River of Lost Souls that lay in the West.

An hour later, the sun now poised atop the horizon, we found a clearing and set about the task of gathering sticks for our fire. Once we had enough, the Prince made some kindling, and creating sparks from two flints, he set them alight. "Now we must gather wood and build our fire," he said as we warmed our hands.

By nightfall, our fire burned brightly enough to illuminate our little clearing. "Our work is not quite done," said the Prince, "we must also make a torch."

"A torch? But the fire is already so bright," I pointed out.

"Just a precaution. It's something we can use to ward off any emboldened wolves."

The Prince made a flaming torch, and steadying it in a hole he'd dug on his left, we sat tethered beside the fire.

"Did you hear that?" I whispered.

"I hear only the crackling of the fire ..." he replied, gazing into it.

"I have no wish to alarm you, but ... there it is again."

"A wolf baying? Yes, I heard it that time—although it sounds at least a league away."

"I can see how even being trapped in that odious tower would prove a comfort on a night like this."

The Prince nodded. "For so long, the wolves have been my only companions. It will sound silly, but ... I used to imagine they were my pets, calling to me. Why do you look at me so?"

"That may be the most desperate thing I've ever heard."

"True," he smiled, "particularly when you consider that my imaginary pets would have devoured me." The Prince shuddered, and crossing my free right hand over my left, I held fast to his arm.

"I don't understand," he mused, resting his head upon my own.

"Understand?"

"How one possessed of such beauty and charity, who could have anyone of their choosing ..."

"Indeed, and I will quite understand if, when all is said and done, you do not choose me."

"And what's more, you have a sense of humour," he said, kissing the top of my head.

I pulled my head away and looked up into his eyes. "Father always says how important it is to laugh at yourself."

"Your father is a wise man."

"He also told me that the eyes are the windows to the soul ..." I said, gazing into his.

"Do you see anything of merit in mine?"

"In both you *and* your brother's. You both have such beautiful souls. Old souls. Even if your brother *has* kept a secret from me. I don't suppose you have any idea what it might be?"

The Prince looked suddenly confused. He cleared his throat nervously and said, "We must continue our journey at first light. I think it best you get a few hours' sleep."

"You do?"

"Yes. You are going to need your wits about you tomorrow."

I closed my eyes and rested my head on his shoulder. "You will wake me at dawn, then?"

"I will."

Journal entry no. 26

I was woken at dawn but not by the Prince, but by the howling of wolves. I felt myself being lifted to my feet and, blinking the sleep from my eyes, I saw the Prince reach down for the burning torch. "What time is it?" I asked.

"The break of dawn ..." said the Prince, holding up the torch and peering at our surrounds for any sign of movement. The fire had burned down to its embers, and dawn's first light now crept into our little clearing. "Let's be on our way," he said, "our torch will continue to burn and provide us protection until the sun has risen."

"And then?"

"Wolves tend only to hunt at night." And so it was that we continued our journey west.

We had not gone far when I heard a sound that caused me to draw a fearful breath—some poor man, *clearly* in great peril, cried out in agony. The Prince and I stopped in our tracks. "The wolves ..." breathed the Prince, "they have set upon someone."

"I have never heard such a pitiable cry! Was it coming from up ahead?"

"There it is again …"

"It did come from up ahead! Come on!" I said, taking hold of his hand and moving forwards. We came to a steep bank, at the bottom of which was a clearing. We looked down to where boulders had been piled high to make a wall—one that snaked away through the forest in both directions. The man shrieked in agony again from beyond the wall. "Come on!" I said, lowering myself onto my backside. The Prince followed suit, and we slid down the embankment to the bottom. We helped each other up gingerly, making certain that the rope remained intact, and no sooner had we got our bearings when a vicious snarling erupted from beyond the wall. There was a small gap in it to our right, and having glanced nervously at one another, we made our way over.

The gap was waist height and barely wide enough for someone to squeeze through. The Prince, aware of my concern, allowed me the first look. I crouched down, and the scene I beheld was so terrible that even recalling it now has set my heart racing and my mind into anguish! On the other side of the wall, the Beast lay on his side, *horribly* bloodied and endeavouring to fend off a pack of wolves, several members of which lay dead upon the ground.

"What is it? What do you see?" asked the Prince.

"It's the Beast! The wolves are *killing* him!" I moved forwards instinctively to reach him and felt the loop tighten about my wrist. The Prince looked up towards the top of the wall. "Maybe … maybe I can throw him the torch over it."

"It's too high!"

"Then what would you have me do?"

"You? But what can you do? You will not fit through this gap! There is only one thing for it …" I said as the Beast cried out in agony.

"And that one thing is?" asked the Prince nervously.

"*I* must go to him," I said, reaching for the burning torch and sliding it from his grasp.

"You … you would break it? You would break our tether for the Beast?"

"Yes! I can't allow him to die! Not like this. I'm sorry, but I just *can't*," I said, sliding my hand free of the loop that secured us. As I did so, the Prince's form began to fade, and the unexpected warmth of his smile as he did so was something that I resolved to remember until my dying day. The next moment, I was squeezing through that gap and pressing forward for all I was worth. When I came out the other side, I beheld the Beast lying on his back, breathing fast, and the remaining wolves, three in number, preparing to finish him off. A protective rage rose within my breast, and brandishing the torch before me, I darted forwards, swinging it at the closest wolf. The flame singed it horribly down one side. It swung around to face me, yelped, stumbled sideways, and then darted away. The remaining two wolves sniffed at the stench of burnt fur and walked cautiously around the now unconscious Beast towards me. Once again, a protective anger rose within me, and I leapt forwards, swinging the torch like a maniac. It struck the snout of one of the wolves with a 'clack!' The creature yelped and retreated while the other circled around behind me. I spun about and ran at it, swinging the torch and yelling like a banshee. The wolf dodged the flame by centimetres but the fur around its neck caught alight, and it darted away. I turned and stepped towards the last wolf, its head held low as it calculated its chances against the fire. Its eyes met my own, and something in my gaze must have convinced it that I meant to protect the Beast come what may. It turned and followed the other into the undergrowth. I lay down the torch, ran to the Beast's side and, kneeling, took his hand in my own. "Please, wake up, you *must* ..." Tears fell from my eyes, and as they splashed upon the Beast's face, he opened his eyes and gazed up at me. "*Beauty?*" he barely breathed.

"Yes, it is I ... you're alive!" I said, clutching his hand ever more tightly.

"You saved me?"

"Yes!"

"But what of the Prince?"

"I was forced to make a choice," I sobbed miserably, "and please don't despise me, but ... my choice has meant that the curse can never be broken now."

"Choice?"

"Yes, and I chose you."

"Me? But why?"

"Why? Isn't it obvious? I *love* you." No sooner had those words passed my lips than the Beast was transformed before my eyes into the Prince.

"But ... I don't understand. Where is the Beast!?"

The Prince drew my hand to his beating heart. "He lies before you ... this hand that holds your own, his paw; this beating heart you feel in my chest, his heart. Don't you see? The Beast and I, we … we are one in the same."

"The *same* …" I breathed, the fog only now beginning to clear.

"Yes, my darling. There were never two brothers," said the Prince, kissing my hand.

"Not two …" I repeated as though waking from a dream.

The Prince sat up and brushed a stray hair from my eyes. "Only one foolish Prince … a Prince who loves you dearly."

"And what of the curse?"

"Broken! Torn asunder by the choice you were forced to make."

"You mean to tell me that … that I have chosen *correctly?*"

The Prince hugged me close. "Yes, Beauty! The curse could only be broken if someone saw through my beastly appearance and fell in love with the man lost within." As the Prince said these words, our surrounds changed into those of the ballroom in his palace. One by one, his servants materialised, until a hundred stood before us, gazing wide-eyed at their own hands. And when the Prince stood and helped me to my feet, they looked on, clapping uproariously. The butler Hobbs, who I could now see to be an upstanding, straight-backed gentleman with a handlebar moustache, stepped forwards, bowed and said, "Welcome home, sir. Words cannot express how good it is to see you again."

"And the same goes for you, Hobbs. For *all* of you," the Prince said with a smile, gazing raptly at his assembled servants. "And we owe it all to this remarkable young woman," he said, squeezing my hand.

"All I did was follow my heart," I said through my blushes.

"I never doubted you. Not for a second," came Betty's familiar voice as she stepped from behind Hobbs and smiled. Over her shoulder, I saw a young woman with long dark hair whom I knew to be Molly. "Hello, Molly," I mouthed.

Molly smiled, waved and curtsied.

I felt the Prince's hand in my own, and as he gently pulled me around to face him, my heart bounded for joy at the thought of what he may be about to do. Sure enough, he fell upon one knee, and having produced a ruby red ring from his waistcoat pocket, he asked if I would do him the honour of becoming his wife.

"Yes! …" I blurted, and the next I knew, the ring was on my finger. The Prince swept me up in his arms and twirled me around that ballroom until it and all its inhabitants became the happiest of blurs …

My final journal entry …

The days that followed were full of wedding arrangements, dress fittings, and happiness. My family came for a visit, and as you might imagine, Father and my brothers were absolutely thrilled for me. On the other hand, my sisters were … well, let's just say they skulked about the palace in a way that reminded me of those singed wolves.

As I write this, my final journal entry, I find myself reflecting on the improving message of my story. My favourite books have always had one. Be that to be braver, kinder, more adventurous, or truer to one's self, etc. Looking back through my own tale, I think its message is clear—to look upon others not only with our eyes but with our hearts. To *listen* to what they have to say and never make snap judgements based on appearances alone.

Betty is the only person in the land who knows about this journal. I read it to her this morning. Indeed, if it does not find its way to the real world in years to come, she will be the only person to hear my tale from the horse's mouth.

"I love it," she said as I finished reading her the entry before this one. "And I think it's a *very* good thing you wrote it."

"Why do you say so?" I asked.

Betty considered her words carefully. "Stories such as yours are generally passed on through word of mouth."

"True. And?"

"And, as is so often the case, it's the menfolk who do the passing."

"And your point?"

"I bet you *anything* you like that in their version, it's the Prince who saves *you* from a pack of ravenous wolves."

"Surely not," I replied, sliding my journal under my bed.

The End

Thank you for reading! If you enjoyed this book, other children's books by
Boyd Brent for the same age group include:

The Lost Diary of Snow White Trilogy
I Am Pan: The Fabled Journal of Peter Pan
Tambourine Jean & The Extraordinary Head Case
Diary of a Wizard Kid 1 & 2

The opening pages to The Lost Diary of Snow White Trilogy follow here …

This diary is the property of Snow White.

Strictly speaking, I'm not supposed to keep a diary. No fairytale characters are. It's *the* unwritten rule of the land. And now I know why: because life here is so unlike anything people in the real world have been led to believe. Once it's finished, I'll have to find a hiding place for it. But if you're holding it now, it means it's been found, and the truth about my life can *finally* be revealed...

Monday

"Mirror, mirror on the wall, who's the fairest of them all?"

"You are Snow White." I've never much cared for this mirror. It's not even supposed to have an opinion – not according to the fairy tale upon which my life is based. It's only my evil stepmother's mirror that's supposed to say what an unrivalled beaut I am. Well, it simply isn't true. I mean, there's pale and then there's PALE. And I'm the kind of PALE that makes me visible from space most nights.

I can't *tell* you what a relief it is to share this secret: you can't believe everything you read in fairy tales. The truth is that all the mirrors in the land (not to mention all the reflective surfaces) are wrong about my fairest-of-them-all status. I caught my reflection in Not Particularly Hopeful's eyes the other day, and his eyes said (you heard me correctly, welcome to my fairytale paradise), "You are without doubt the fairest of them all, Snow White." At this point you may be wondering who Not Particularly Hopeful is. You know there are seven dwarves, and even though you can't name them all, you're pretty certain that none of them are called Not Particularly Hopeful. Yet another misunderstanding about my life. There are *five* dwarves, and contrary to popular belief, none are even remotely Happy. How could they be, with names like Not Particularly Hopeful, Insecure, Meddlesome, Inconsolable and Awkward? According to the little lamb that skips past my kitchen window every morning, the dwarves represent facets of my own personality. Cripes.

That's deep. Particularly for a constantly-on-the-go lamb of such tiny proportions.

Then there's Prince Charming. He wasn't supposed to arrive until *after* my stepmother poisons me, and I've been in a coma for a hundred years. As the story goes, that's when he wakes me with a kiss, and after that we live happily ever after. No pressure, then. But the other day, when the little lamb hopped, skipped and jumped past my kitchen window, it bleated something about a hunky prince on a white stallion coming into my life. "Really?" I replied. "Stop the press. We're talking in a hundred years' time, once I'm fully rested and up to the challenge of living happily ever after."

"No," replied the little lamb. "His arrival is imminent."

"Imminent?"

"Any second now."

"Did you swallow a dictionary? Imminent? I don't think…" And there he was, a hunky prince riding a white stallion. He looked me up and down, smiled and said, "Reports of your beauty have not been exaggerated. You are indeed the fairest in the land." Prince Charming isn't the only one who can look a person up and down. And once I'd made a point of doing just that – minus the smile, of course – I said, "What are you *doing* here? You're over a century early. Please. Leave me alone. I'm not ready to live happily ever after yet."

"Nonsense!" said he. "One so perfect on the outside must also be perfect on the inside. And ready for any challenge. What have you to say to that?"

"That you should never judge a book by its cover," said I firmly.

As Prince Charming rode away on his horse, he called out, "I intend to win you over, Snow."

"But why ever would you want to?"

"So we can live happily ever after."

"Really? No pressure, then!"

The next day as I swept the porch, the little lamb saw me crying. It hopped about in a circle and bleated, "Whatever is your problem?" I rested my chin on the broom handle, and my eyes went up and down as they followed its cute bounce. "My problem? At least I can do stationary. What's with all the bouncing, anyway?"

"I was just written this way: always on the move, and quite unable to slow down."

"Really? Well, I was just written this way."

"What way?" asked the little lamb.

"I suppose I'm insecure. And at times such as these, quite inconsolable."

"Anything else?"

"Well, now you come to mention it, I'm awkward and not particularly hopeful."

"About what?"

"About living happily ever after with the prince."

"Why? Is the prince not charming by name *and* by nature?"

"I presume so. But he doesn't understand me at all."

"Then introduce the prince to your dwarves. The clues are in their names," said the wise little lamb.

I began sweeping the porch again and said, "First of all, they aren't *my* dwarves, and secondly the prince is already well acquainted with them."

"Then he's been blinded by your beauty?"

I nodded mournfully, then shook my head. "He must need his eyes tested. I have seen a three-headed toad fairer than I."

Saturday

Today my evil stepmother invited me to tea. Yes, that's right, the same evil stepmother who has hated me ever since she asked her mirror, "Who's the fairest in the land?" and it lied and told her that I was. And ever since that day, she's been trying to poison me with apples. She's quite the one-trick pony in that way: apples, apples, always apples. My friend Cinderella said I should count my blessings.

"Blessings?" said I.

"Yes. That your stepmother has absolutely no imagination when it comes to poisoning you." Cinders also pointed out that I'm related to my stepmother. And that when it comes to our relatives, we must make allowances, even if they do hate us enough to poison us with fruit. Then she reminded me of what she has to put up with with her sisters. Poor Cinders. They give her a dreadful time.

My stepmother sent a sparrow with a message this morning. In between tweets, the sparrow read the following to me: 'I'm so excited about your early engagement! You must come for tea! And a slice of apple pie! I baked it myself only this morning! Especially for you!" As you can see, my stepmother is fond of exclamation marks. In my experience, the more exclamation marks a person uses, the crazier they are. It's really no different from someone shouting all the time for no apparent reason.

I stepped onto the porch, and whistled for Barry the boar. Barry runs a taxi service, and is the fastest boar in the land (ask any mirror). He also has the longest tusks, and they're perfect to hang on to. "Mind that hanging branch, Barry!" said I, lowering my head.

"I see it."

"Appreciate the ride, Baz."

"No problem, Snow. Happy to help out. How are the dwarves? Still whistling while they work?"

"Oh, yes. Of course. It helps to keep their spirits up. It's hard work down that mine."

"If I could, I'd whistle while I worked too."

"Then why don't you?"

"I can't on account of my piggy lips. Whenever I try, I blow raspberries instead."

Barry dropped me off outside the palace, and then trotted off, blowing raspberries (at least, I assume he was trying to whistle). And so it was with a heavy heart that I turned and knocked on the door. The palace is very large and the butler very small. The sun had gone down by the time he let me in... and had risen again by the time we reached the parlour, where my stepmother stood over an apple pie, pastry knife in hand. "Pie?" she asked.

"I'll take a rain check on the pie, thank you."

"Nonsense," said she, cutting an ample slice. "You're such a waif of a thing. You need fattening up."

"Oh," I said, looking at my reflection in one of the parlour's many mirrors. "I'm quite fat enough already, thank you."

My stepmother slammed the knife down on the table. "Fat, are you? If you're *fat,* then what does that make me?" She turned yellow and green with envy (she does that a lot around me), then she remembered her charm offensive and assumed a more plausible colour. "No matter," said she. "How lovely it is to see you! I so look forward to your visits. Come and sit beside me. Tell me all about Prince Charming. He must be awfully keen. Why else would he turn up so early?"

I sat down, and she placed a piece of pie before me on a plate. I watched as apple oozed from its sides.

"What*ever* is the matter? It won't bite," she said.

I pushed the plate away. "I'm too bloated for pie. And what's more, I don't want to marry Prince Charming. Not yet."

"Why ever not?"

"Because I'm not ready to live happily ever after."

My stepmother rang a little bell on the table to summon a servant. "We'll skip the apple pie," she told her servant, "and have apple strudel instead."

I rolled my eyes.

My stepmother did the same, then she lowered her voice to a whisper and said, "Trust me. If you have a slice of my apple strudel, you won't have to marry the prince."

"Oh? And why is that?"

"Because it's an enchanted strudel," she whispered, like she was confiding a secret. *You mean because it's a poisoned strudel,* I thought. I straightened my back and said, "I'm in no need of enchantment at the moment, thank you very much."

"Ungrateful girl!"

"Is my father home?"

"The king is away on state business."

"Will he be back soon?"

"Just as soon as you eat some strudel."

"I won't do it," said I.

"How about a nice bowl of fruit salad?"

"Are there apples in it?"

"Just the one."

"No, thank you."

"Toffee apple?"

"No."

"Apple fritter?"

"No."

"Tart, then."

"Ex*cuse* me?"

"Apple tart?"

"No way."

"Perhaps I can tempt you with a delicious glass of apple cider? Seventy percent proof. Promise I won't tell your father."

I couldn't take any more apple offers, I simply couldn't. So I left.

It was cold and dark, and a long walk back to my cottage. I felt a pang of guilt at not being home to make the dwarves their supper. After all, they had taken me in and befriended me in my hour of need. It seems like only yesterday when my stepmother asked her mirror *that* question, and it lied to her. She told the woodcutter to take me into the woods and make sure that I *never* came back. I promised the woodcutter that if he let me go, I would leave the land for good. And that way, my stepmother's mirror would tell her that *she* was the fairest in all the land. The woodcutter must have been a kindly fellow, for he let me go. I walked for many days looking everywhere for the exit to the land, but the land seemed to go on forever. I grew downcast, and that's when I came upon the dwarves. They were on their way home after a hard day down the mine. "Excuse me," I said. "I have been walking for days, and I'm very tired. I'm looking for an exit to the land. Is it close by?"

Not Particularly Hopeful shook his head (I've since discovered that Not Particularly Hopeful shakes his head a lot), then Inconsolable began to cry. I put my arm around the little fellow, doing my best to console him, but it was quite useless. Awkward went bright red and snorted... awkwardly. He looked at Insecure, who said not to ask him *anything* because he didn't know anything. Not Particularly Hopeful spoke up again, and he said that as far he knew, there was no exit to the land. Not anywhere. That everywhere you went, you found more land. And there you had it. Or didn't. Not if you were looking for an exit, anyway.

I sat down on a tree stump and rested my heavy head in my hands. "Do you mean to say that I've spent all this time looking for something that doesn't exist?"

Inconsolable blew his nose, and said it wasn't like it had stopped anybody before. So why should it stop me? Then he pointed in no direction in particular and said the exit was probably that way.

"It can't be. Not if it doesn't exist. Oh, whatever I shall I do! I promised the woodcutter."

"Can you cook?" asked Meddlesome. "Only, Insecure makes all our meals and he's a terrible cook."

Insecure nodded his head in agreement.

"I suppose I can cook. I won't really know until I try," I said.

"What about housework?" asked Meddlesome. "Only, Insecure does all our housework too, and he's terrible at it."

Again, Insecure nodded.

"I suppose I could do housework. I won't really know until I try."

The dwarves went into a huddle, and they decided that in return for cooking and cleaning, I would be given a roof over my head. Apparently, I was almost exactly what they'd been looking for.

The early hours of Sunday morning…

So anyway, back to the present. As you may recall, I'd just left my stepmother's, and had begun my walk home in the dark through the woods. I was just feeling peckish (for just about anything other than apple) when I saw a trail of breadcrumbs. The trail was long and winding, and once I'd eaten it, I found myself on my hands and knees outside a cottage – not my own cottage, but one made entirely from gingerbread. I said to myself, "*Dessert?* I like gingerbread, but don't think I could eat a whole abode."

I peered in through a kitchen window. Inside, I saw a small boy sitting beside a sweet old lady. The old lady was feeding him marshmallows by hand. *How lovely,* I thought. I heard someone chopping wood close by, and hoped it might be the woodcutter. I felt guilty about breaking my promise to him, and wanted to explain why I hadn't left the land. *The land is absolutely everywhere,* I would say. *And therefore quite impossible to leave. And if you did, you'd end up precisely nowhere. And how dreadful would that be?* Having rehearsed my explanation in my mind, and being happy with it, I was disappointed to see not the woodcutter, but a little girl chopping wood. She had long brown hair and big brown eyes, and said her name was Gretel. As it turned out, Gretel and I had a lot in common: she had a stepmother of questionable character too. Her stepmother had left her in the woods with her brother Hansel, where she hoped they would starve to death.

"That's pretty grim," I said.

She nodded and asked, "Did your stepmother abandon you to starve in the woods as well?"

"Oh, no. She told the woodcutter to flat-out murder me." I glanced over my shoulder at the gingerbread house. "Thank goodness," I said.

"What do you mean?" she asked.

"That you and your brother found a happy ending after all."

"How so?"

"You came upon a lovely gingerbread house. And a kind old lady who feeds children marshmallows by hand."

Gretel shook her head. "She's not a kind old lady. She's a witch. And she's fattening my brother up."

"But why?"

"So there'll be ample meat on his bones when she eats him. Or so she said."

I tutted.

Gretel echoed my tut and said, "The old witch plans to fatten me up too, and then she's going to eat me. But not before she's worked my fingers to the bone." I reached out and squeezed Gretel's shoulder. "Sorry. That's pretty rough. Whatever does a person have to do to get a break in this land?"

"It beats me," said she.

"I won't have it."

Gretel shrugged her shoulders. "What can you do? What can anybody do? It's just the way our story was written."

"I used to think that way too. And then my prince arrived early, and said he couldn't wait to marry me."

"You must have been so happy," sighed Gretel.

I cast my gaze upon the ground and shook my head. "I'm not ready to live happily ever after. Tell me, is there any mention of me in your story?"

"Who are you?"

"Snow White."

"The fairest in the land?"

I shook my head.

"Well, no," said Gretel. "I don't believe there's any mention of Snow White."

I folded my arms and said, "My own story has been changed. And my being here only goes to prove one thing."

"And that is?" asked Gretel.

I raised an arm and brought my thumb and forefinger together. "That we might change it a *teensy weensy* bit more."

"How so?"

My gaze fell upon the axe in her hands, then I looked over my shoulder at the cottage where the witch was fattening up her brother.

"Oh!" said Gretel. "Why ever didn't I think of that?"

Monday

I'm back at home now, and you'll be pleased to know that
Hansel and Gretel's story ended happily after all. The same
could not be said for the witch. I imagine she had quite a
shock when Gretel burst into her kitchen, axe raised above
her head, and said the story was about to be altered 'a *teensy
weensy* bit more.'

Today Prince Charming invited me to the enchanted lake for
a picnic. He seems quite convinced that he can change my
mind about marrying him early. His invite said that when it
came to wooing the ladies his record was flawless. And that
even if he had to make an effort to understand my feelings,
that's precisely what he would do. His message said I should
fear not and *brace myself for falling hopelessly in love*, and
that if all else fails, *I should get a grip for once in my life.*

I handed the dwarves their lunch boxes and kissed them
goodbye at the garden gate – all except Insecure, who was
even more worried than usual about hitting the wrong part of
the mine and causing a cave-in. "I'll stay with you today,
Snow, that's if you don't mind?" Of all my dwarves, I feel
closest to Insecure. "Of course I don't mind. I'm going to
meet Prince Charming down at the enchanted lake later."

"Do you mind if I tag along?" he asked.

"You know, I somehow thought you might."

Insecure and I walked up a steep hill, on the other side of
which the sun glistened upon an enchanted lake and leaves
rustled upon enchanted tress. At the top of the hill, we

stopped and looked down upon the scene as just described. The only difference was Prince Charming. He lay on a blanket beneath the shade of a tall tree, his perfect head placed in a perfect palm, a blade of grass turning slowly between his perfect lips. Placed upon his blanket were all manner of tasty treats to tempt me.

Insecure looked up at me and I looked down at Insecure. "The prince will not be at all happy to see me," said he. "Of that I'm quite sure."

"What makes you say that?" asked I.

Insecure sat down and hugged his knees to his chest. "Because nobody is ever happy to see me. I'll keep watch over you from up here."

"If you're sure?"

Insecure nodded.

"Okay then."

As I approached the prince, he got up and told me I grew fairer with each visit. "Come and sit beside me," said he, "and share this delightful picnic."

Prince Charming and I sat cross-legged opposite each another. He took an apple from a bowl of fruit and handed it to me. "The apple's ruddiness is intense, is it not?" said he. I glanced down at the apple in my hand. Indeed, it was the ruddiest apple I had ever seen. The prince smiled and said, "I chose that apple for you especially."

"Why?"

"Because it matches perfectly the colour of your cheeks when you blush."

"Really? Thanks. I think."

"Tell me," said he, leaning closer, "what good and charitable deeds have you performed lately?"

I rubbed the apple against my sleeve to bring out its shine. "What makes you think I've performed any good and charitable deeds?"

"One as fair as you must have charity in her heart."

"Really? Well…"

"Come now, my love, there's no need to be coy about your charitable deeds."

I took a bite out of the apple. As I chewed I said, "I presume my stepmother didn't provide the fruit for this picnic?"

Prince Charming's eyes opened wide, and they filled with wonder. "Not only are you the fairest in the land, you also possess the wisdom of kings."

With a mouthful of apple it wasn't easy to talk, but I did my best. "Are you 'elling me that eye step-um gave 'ou this apple?"

"Yes, my darling. She insisted on supplying all the fruit for our picnic."

I spat out the apple. As I picked bits of it out of his hair and lap, I said, "In the future, if my stepmother offers you fruit… say no."

"But why, my love?"

"She's been trying to poison me with it for years."

"With *fruit*?"

"Apples, to be precise."

"I can't believe *anyone* would wish to harm even a hair on your fair head."

"Believe it."

"I don't want to believe it."

"You must believe it."

"But what if I can't believe it?"

"Then you must try harder."

"But why apples, my darling?"

I shrugged up my heavy shoulders. "Maybe she's just written that way." Prince Charming stood up and hurled the fruit bowl into the enchanted lake. Moments later, a great many fish floated to its surface, all in deep comas from which they would never awaken – well, not unless kissed by a prince who wanted to live happily ever after with a fish. I thought about how unlikely this was, and sighed.

Prince Charming sat down again. "Now," said he, "you were about to tell me of your charitable deeds?"

"But why should I?"

Prince Charming leaned back on the palms of his hands. "I have been led to believe that talking of your charitable deeds will fill you with pride, and make you feel less insecure."

I leaned back on my own palms. "Fat to no chance of that," said I.

"All the same, please indulge me."

"Alright. I helped a brother and sister in the woods yesterday. Does that count?"

"I knew it! One so fair must carry out at least *one* charitable deed every single day."

"If you say so."

"Tell me of these fortunate siblings whose paths crossed your own, my dearest, most charitable darling."

"I simply had to help them."

"Oh, my darling!"

"We had such a lot in common."

"How so?"

"They have a stepmother of questionable character too."

"So how did you come upon the unfortunate brother and sister?"

"Their names were Hansel and Gretel. I came upon Gretel chopping wood. She told me how a witch was fattening her brother for her cooking pot."

The prince looked suitably concerned and said, "Whatever does a person have to do to get a break in this land?"

"Tell me about it."

"So what did you do?" asked the prince.

"Well, I knew I had to change their story, as mine had been changed."

"And?"

"And I considered the options available to me."

"Very wise, my love, very wise indeed. And these options were?"

"Pretty scarce, actually. There was a barn filled to bursting with marshmallows, a well filled with chocolate syrup, and a young girl with a grudge... and armed with an axe."

The prince twirled his moustache and looked very pleased with himself. "Say no more," said he. "It's clear that your plan involved marshmallows and chocolate syrup."

Thank you for reading! If you enjoyed this sample, *The Lost Diary of Snow White Trilogy* is available from Amazon.

19956561R00109

Made in the USA
Middletown, DE
08 December 2018